"THIS IS HOPELESS, ZACH," DARA SAID. "WE weren't compatible as kids, and we're even more incompatible now. You leap before you look, and most of the time I don't even make it to the edge."

"You're wrong. The reason we didn't get along as kids was because we were too much alike. You're still one of the bravest people I know."

"You know what I'm saying, Zach," she persisted. "You keep thinking of me the way I was back then. I'm not that person anymore. You're still impulsive, I'm not. You're—"

"Getting tired of this line of discussion." He sighed and pulled her closer. "Yes, you've changed. So have I, even if you don't see it. I don't know why you climbed into the castle and pulled up the drawbridge behind you, but that doesn't mean we shouldn't spend time together. Who knows, maybe we'll find out there's something more going on here than hormones with a bad case of spring fever." He tilted her chin up. "Or is that what you're afraid of?"

WHAT ARE *LOVESWEPT* ROMANCES?

They are stories of true romance and touching emotion. We believe those two very important ingredients are constants in our highly sensual and very believable stories in the LOVE-SWEPT line. Our goal is to give you, the reader, stories of consistently high quality that may sometimes make you laugh, sometimes make you cry, but are always fresh and creative and contain many delightful surprises within their pages.

Most romance fans read an enormous number of books. Those they truly love, they keep. Others may be traded with friends and soon forgotten. We hope that each LOVESWEPT romance will be a treasure—a "keeper." We will always try to publish

LOVE STORIES YOU'LL NEVER FORGET
BY AUTHORS YOU'LL ALWAYS REMEMBER

The Editors

Loveswept®⁷⁷¹

The Three Musketeers:

BORN TO
BE WILD

DONNA
KAUFFMAN

BANTAM BOOKS
NEW YORK · TORONTO · LONDON · SYDNEY · AUCKLAND

BORN TO BE WILD

A Bantam Book / January 1996

ISBN 0-553-44470-0

Published simultaneously in the United States and Canada

Bantam Books are published by Bantam Books, a division of Bantam Dou-
bleday Dell Publishing Group, Inc. Its trademark, consisting of the words
"Bantam Books" and the portrayal of a rooster, is Registered in U.S. Patent
and Trademark Office and in other countries. Marca Registrada. Bantam
Books, 1540 Broadway, New York, New York 10036.

PRINTED IN THE UNITED STATES OF AMERICA

OPM   0 9 8 7 6 5 4 3 2 1

This book is dedicated to
Debra Dixon.
Because Swami Debbie is never wrong.

PROLOGUE

He plummeted toward the earth.

Zach Brogan arched his back, thrusting his chest and hips forward. Cool air buffeted his body as a familiar inner heat rapidly consumed him, making his fingertips tingle and his toes curl. He savored the incredibly odd dual sensations of feeling both weightless and stone-heavy while the ground rushed up to meet him.

God, this was almost better than sex.

The never-ending vista of arid, desolate landscape lay fully exposed below him, and his mind seized every detail, living each second of the free fall to the fullest.

The Atacama Desert in northern Chile wasn't the most hospitable place in the world and probably ranked about dead last as a vacation locale. Unless, of course, you enjoyed the challenge of finding your way out of a cold desert with little or no resources except your skill as a survivor.

For Zach, the land below was his own version of Disneyland. Deserts, mountains, volcanoes, mild rain forest vegetation, rugged steep cliffs that hugged the ocean, all courtesy of one country. A thrill-seeker's paradise.

"Hot damn, this is a rush!"

The words crackled across the stratosphere into the headphones inside Zach's helmet. The addictive intimacy of those first few moments of free flight dissolved, and Zach let it go without remorse. He'd felt it before. He'd feel it again.

The broad grin came naturally as he shot a thumbs-up to the man falling through space beside him, automatically running a mental checkup on his client's position. Posture good. Chute release properly positioned between his fingers.

Zach lowered his chin and spoke into the small microphone. "Two seconds."

The man next to him nodded and returned the thumbs-up. A breath later he disappeared from sight. Up, up, and away.

Zach rolled and looked up into the startling blue afternoon sky, making sure the canopy and pilot chute had opened properly and that Cortinez was following correct procedure, then returned his attention to the ground.

He should pull now, but he didn't. Pushing, pushing . . . Another hot rush stole over his skin; his pulse pounded, he grew hard.

At the last possible moment he yanked the cord.

ONE

Today her dream job had all the makings of a perfect nightmare. Dara Colbourne rushed down the hallway to her office. "I should have known better than to stop off at Cavendish's office on the way in." She swore under her breath, a common occurrence after a meeting with Dream A Little Dream's founder. "That man gives new meaning to the term benevolent dictator."

She shifted the pile of folders threatening to topple from her arms, careful not to jostle the cup of now-cold coffee in her hand. She'd hoped to go over her notes one last time before confronting her first appointment. And a confrontation it was likely to be. Having the upper hand right from the start was imperative if she was to get this over with quickly.

Of course, during their history together she'd never once had the upper hand with him, but she was a firm believer in positive thinking. Besides, a lot could change in fifteen years.

"Please, let him be soft and slow," she muttered,

knowing that particular prayer wouldn't be answered but asking anyway. "And late."

Using her hip, she bumped open the door. It moved two inches, hit something solid and swung swiftly backward. Directly into her coffee cup.

"Oh!" The cold brew soaked through her favorite white silk shirt. Her once-favorite white silk shirt, she amended silently, staring down at the blotchy brown mess.

Her office door swung open again, and a tall, broad body filled the entrance. Biting down on a curse, Dara looked up. Past faded, dusty jeans that became increasingly formfitting, past the black T-shirt tucked snugly enough to showcase the flat abdomen it covered, past the words "No Fear Gear" scrawled in electric blue across a vast expanse of hard-muscled chest, past the tanned neck framed with unruly blond hair, and came to rest on the pair of mischief-filled brown eyes that had haunted her throughout her childhood.

Eyes she'd once thought—hoped, prayed fervently even—she'd never have to see again.

The cold coffee dripped between her breasts and trickled out beneath her bra to track down her stomach. "Zach Brogan." She smiled dryly. "How nice to see you again."

His wink was as sexy as it was audacious. "Sure you saw enough?"

The voice was still teasing, but rather than high-pitched and ornery, it was low and dark. Not sounding remotely like the teenager he'd been the last time she'd seen him. So much for soft or slow.

"I can show you more if you like," he added easily.

His grin spread, flashing even rows of perfect white teeth. It was nothing short of astonishing just how incredibly generous Mother Nature had been to him.

More proof that life wasn't fair.

A truth she worked to change every day, and one she doubted he had even a passing acquaintance with.

"Well," she said with studied nonchalance. "The body has improved, Brogan. But the mind is still in grade school."

He made a sizzling sound and shot her a mock wounded look. "Little Dart. Still a fire-breather, I see." Zach lifted the pile of folders from her arms without asking, the unwieldy stack looking somehow small and manageable in his big arms. "It's been a long time." He inclined his head, motioning her into the office ahead of him.

"Fifteen years," she responded, moving quickly past him.

"Seems hard to believe we never bumped into each other in all that time."

It wasn't hard for her to believe. She'd been fifteen when her mother had remarried and they'd moved from Madison County to Fairfax. Both counties were in the state of Virginia, not fifty miles apart, but back then it had seemed a galaxy away. Her twin brother, Dane, had worked hard over the years to maintain his friendship with Zach.

Dara had just thanked her lucky stars to be rid of him.

She heard him close the door behind her. "We don't exactly move in the same circles," she said finally, not really wanting to get into their particular past.

"No. I don't imagine you travel in a circle at all. More of a straight-line type, I hear."

The underlying edge in his statement caught her off guard, but she managed to swallow the retort that sprang to her lips. After all, she wasn't an awkward teenager any longer. She could hold her own against the likes of one Zach Brogan without resorting to childish one-upmanship.

Leaving him by the door, she walked directly to her desk, grabbing the box of tissues sitting on one corner. His gaze on her back was a tangible thing, and she was surprised at the instant of awareness the knowledge provoked in her. It took an annoying bit of extra concentration to keep her hands steady.

Of all the emotions she'd have expected to feel upon facing her childhood tormentor again, sexual awareness hadn't even made the list. Oh, Dane had kept her informed over the years of just how charming and dashing all the ladies thought Zach to be. But that had been the case all through school, beginning with kindergarten when he'd wrapped poor Mrs. Potter around his then-pudgy pinky finger by asking her to marry him on the second day of class.

Dara, on the other hand, had been completely immune to it—inoculated early on by his endless pranks at her expense—and she really hadn't imagined time would change that. His globe-trotting, wild man lifestyle might seem exciting and exotic to some women, but Dara was no longer drawn to bold, larger-than-life males. It had taken several painful lessons for it to sink in, beginning when she was eleven and her much-adored pilot father had died, and finally, mercifully, ending with the death of her athlete fiancé when she was in college.

Bold and brash may have enticed her when she was young; she'd been quite the daredevil herself as a kid. But that was then. She'd grown up and entered the real world. And she'd never looked back.

She certainly didn't plan to now.

The stack of folders appeared on her desk as she dabbed at the sticky mess on the front of her shirt, jerking her thoughts back to the present. She felt his warm breath on her neck an instant before he spoke.

"I'd help you with that," Zach said, his deep voice touched with humor, "but I bet Dane we'd go ten minutes before you slugged me, and I don't want to lose twenty bucks."

The tissue she'd been pulling from the box ripped in half at the sudden jerk of her hand. "Your money's safe," she said after a moment, hating the smile that threatened. "I can handle it," she added, hoping she wasn't lying. Yanking a wad of tissues from the box, she edged away from him, dabbing at her blouse while she moved behind her desk.

She'd just made the mistake of thinking of him the way he'd been the last time she'd seen him; an immature teenager just discovering the joys of testosterone. She stupidly hadn't factored in the reality that he was now a man full grown. A man who likely knew just what to do with all that testosterone.

Steadfastly ignoring the responding tingle that idea brought on, she looked down and swiftly rearranged the stack of folders on her desk. "Please, have a seat."

He brushed off the back of his jeans and sat in one of the padded leather chairs across the desk, his huge frame dwarfing the hand-tooled seat.

Catching her looking at the fine layer of dust he'd just sent sifting to her Persian rug, he smiled and shrugged. "Desert dust. The Chilean airstrip I used didn't exactly come equipped with a changing room. And once I hit Dulles, I figured I was beyond redemption." His grin made it clear he wasn't the least disturbed by that notion.

Beyond redemption. Even dusty with a day or two's growth of beard, she was forced to admit he was sexier than sin. And the devil himself would kill for that smile.

She ignored it. "I appreciate your making it here today," she said, putting all the poised professionalism she'd earned over the last eight years into her voice.

His raised eyebrow questioned her sincerity, but all he said was, "I understand you have a problem with using my company, The Great Escape, in conjunction with a donation made to the foundation."

"It's not personal, Zach. Really."

His smile was as dry as the desert dust coating her carpet. "Really."

"Really," she repeated, her tone sharper than intended.

"Well, that certainly explains why I had to scramble to get someone to replace me in the middle of a trip—a very complex, expensive, prepaid trip I might add—because you refused to deal with anyone but me."

"I had no choice. You know the donor specifically requested you to run the trip he's funding. Dream A

Little Dream Foundation relies solely on private donations to fund the granting of wishes made by handicapped and terminally ill children. Occasionally a donation is made for a specific wish, which is the case this time. You have to understand how important it is that every aspect of each wish we decide to fulfill be thoroughly checked."

Zach stretched out his long legs and crossed his arms. "This was all explained to my assistant. I know she provided you with everything you requested. What exactly is the problem?"

"My research has raised some serious questions, and I thought it was important to give you the chance to discuss them before I present my report to the board this afternoon."

"And if I hadn't shown up?" His tone seemed sincere enough, but his lazy sprawl suggested he wasn't overly concerned.

"I can't speak for the board, but I imagine they would have postponed this particular wish request until we could contact the donor and get his approval for another outfitter."

Zach looked confident. Too confident. "I don't think you're going to have much luck contacting the donor anytime soon."

Dara sighed. He knew about Jarrett. She hadn't been sure, but it didn't really surprise her. Though they didn't see each other often, Jarrett McCullough, her brother, Dane, and Zach, were still good friends.

As children they'd been known as the Three Musketeers of Madison County. Dara's constant bid for and continual humiliating failure to gain acceptance into the group as the fourth musketeer is what led Zach to brand her with the nickname Dart. Short for D'Artagnan. Short, because that's what she'd been. Short, scrawny, and for the entire fifteen years they'd lived in Madison County, generally considered by the trio to be a major pain in the butt.

"How did you find out?" she asked. "Did he tell you?"

"Actually, no. I didn't know anything about it until Beaudine contacted me in Chile about this meeting."

"I guess I don't have to tell you why he requested anonymity." Dara knew that up until his wedding a month ago, Jarrett had run a courier service that specialized in handling sensitive information. Usually dealing with thwarting various terrorist activities. His wife, Rae, had been one of his top couriers. "I know he's only consulting now," she went on. "But I guess with Rae and Jarrett out of the country on their honeymoon, they can't be too careful. No one knows where they are, not even Dane."

Zach shrugged. "Me either."

"So how did you find—?"

Zach's raised hand stopped her. "Beaudine has contacts that would scare the President. I didn't ask how. But I didn't question it either."

The name Beaudine Delacroix had come up occasionally when Dane forced her to listen to the wild recounting of his and Jarrett's annual break from sanity which Zach planned for them every summer. She'd never met her, but from everything she'd heard, Dara concluded the woman was nothing short of amazing. Sort of a Cajun Mrs. Doubtfire.

"I did try to contact Jarrett myself," Zach said. "By then even Beaudine couldn't get an exact location on them." He raked one hand through his hair, making it look even wilder than it had before, something she hadn't thought possible.

Her gaze dropped back to his, and the dark intensity she found there was completely at odds with his I-couldn't-give-a-damn attitude.

"Are you really willing to let these kids wait for their camping trip until Jarrett and Rae surface?" He settled his arms back across his chest and crossed his ankles. "I'm pretty booked up, but I've got the manpower and can probably rearrange things enough to get this in within a month or so."

Dara wasn't fooled now. His relaxed posture was simply a calculated move to get her to drop her guard. Zach might be a crazy man, but one look in his eyes proved he was far from stupid.

She took a steadying breath. She had to get him to see this from her point of view. "Zach," she began, "surely you understand why we can't have Great Escape run this trip?"

To her increased annoyance, she realized his attention had wandered—to her blouse. Specifically the part that was plastered to her chest. Her body reacted in an alarmingly instant and very visible manner.

She leaned forward on folded arms, not caring that she was dripping coffee on her sleeves and her desktop, steadfastly ignoring the knowing twinkle in his eyes as his attention shifted back to her face.

Lord, but it was getting harder and harder to keep her train of thought on the same path for more than two minutes.

"Zach," she began again, determined to end this swiftly. "Let's face it. You're not a typical outfitter."

His grin was as wild as his hair. "Yeah, I know."

Dara sighed for what felt like the hundredth time. The man was incorrigible. "I wasn't exactly complimenting you. You're a thrill-seeker. Your company caters to people who think intentionally courting death is fun. Your idea of a good time is skydiving into active volcanoes and hang gliding off of glaciers, for crying out loud."

"Don't forget diving in shark-infested waters," he added with sincerity. The padded leather creaked as he leaned forward. "You keeping tabs on me, Dart?" Another lazy grin curved his lips. "I didn't think you cared."

Talk about shark-infested waters. *I won't let him get to me*, she repeated silently like a mantra.

Of course, it would be a whole lot easier if he didn't sit there looking so damn . . . healthy. And if that deep voice of his didn't make her feel so incredibly . . . aware. And just when she'd get him pegged as nothing more than an outrageous flirt, that sharp edge would appear in his eyes, making her wonder just what sort of thoughts were really lurking behind them.

She gave herself a mental shake, and forced herself to remember the first time she'd let him goad her into acting rashly. She'd been six when Zach had dared her to climb to the top of the monkey bars. He'd waited until she was balanced on the top rung to comment on what a pretty dress she had on, and that he couldn't recall her ever wearing a dress before.

Of course, it was Dara who got sent to the principal's office for decking Zach in the eye. She could still recall the devilish gleam winking out of the other one as she was escorted from the playground. She was looking at the adult replica of that gleam right now.

"No," she said firmly, "I haven't been keeping tabs on you. But Dane forces me to listen to a blow by blow description of the insanity you drag him on every summer."

"You weren't exactly the tame sort, if I recall," he said. "Weren't you the one who used to dare me to climb old Mrs. Prubody's tree and toss rocks at her window? And what about the time you conned Dane, Jarrett, and me into papering the houses of the two head cheerleaders after you were cut from the junior squad?" The gleam in his eyes briefly erupted into a devilish twinkle as he added, "And what was the reason again?" He snapped his fingers. "Oh yeah, something about a catfight you had with a cheerleader from our rival high school, wasn't it?"

She worked hard not to squirm as memories she'd purposely ignored flooded back into her brain. "First of all, she deserved more than getting her hair pulled," Dara retorted, unable to curb her tongue. "And you weren't much of a champion. You took her to the homecoming dance if I recall." She clamped her mouth shut when his grin widened. Then after a deep, calming breath, she said, "But that was a long time ago. We were kids. I've grown up."

The twinkle disappeared. "So," he said too quietly, "based on the assumption that I'm an immature, irresponsible lunatic, you want me to back out of this?"

She shivered. And any hope she had that he'd assume it was simply a result of the cold coffee soaking her blouse was removed by the deepening curve of his mouth. His smile didn't reach his eyes, though. The combination was downright disconcerting.

"It isn't just an assumption," she stated, determined to regain the control she'd somehow lost the moment he'd sat down. "I did some preliminary investigating, and I don't think your company is suitable for the job." She held up her hand to forestall his imminent rebuttal. "Zach, come on. Most kids think they're going to live forever."

"We sure as hell did."

"That's just my point. These kids have known almost right from the start just how precious life is, and they struggle every day just to maintain their grasp on it. You, on the other hand, still think you are immortal. You're like . . ." She lifted her hand, then flattened it palm down on her desk. "You're like Peter Pan with an American Gladiator complex." She leaned forward. "Do you seriously think you're the man to chaperon four children with very special needs on a mountain excursion?"

"To hear you tell it, I can't take anything seriously. So why ask?" He stood with surprising speed and braced his hands on her desk. "You never had any intention of letting me run this trip. This whole thing is really just a formality, isn't it, *Ms. Colbourne?*"

His teasing smile was long gone, his unshaven jaw

rock-hard, lending an air of ruggedness that only enhanced his sex appeal. She hated herself for noticing.

"You're just following procedure, right?" he went on. "I came halfway around the globe because you needed my signature on a formal refusal form, which will allow you to line up some other board-approved outfitter the second you locate McCullough. I wouldn't be surprised if the new guy's appointment is right after mine."

His intensity was palpable, almost frightening. Having all that energy and vitality harnessed and focused solely on her was quite overwhelming, and it took her a few seconds to find an appropriate response.

"There is no other outfitter," she said when she finally found her voice. *Not yet, anyway.* "I wouldn't do that." His snort brought more than a frown to her lips, but she swallowed it at the last possible second. She took a deep breath and looked him in the eye. "But the truth is, I don't think you should run this trip, and, yes, I would appreciate it if you would formally decline."

He leaned farther over her desk, his voice dark and ominously low. "If you really believe that I'd actually put those kids in danger, then maybe it is better to wait for Jarrett to come back and okay a switch." His demeanor was hard and tough and completely foreign to her perception of him.

He straightened. "Can I ask you something?" His tone was deceptively gentle.

"What?" she asked warily.

"Jarrett and Dane stay in fairly close contact, so I imagine you've seen Jarrett occasionally over the years or keep up with what he's doing through Dane, right?"

Her brows furrowed in confusion. "Right."

"You know Dane would trust Jarrett with his life?"

"Yes, but—"

"So would I. And the feeling is mutual."

"I don't see what—"

"Do you trust Jarrett, Dara?"

His tone was insistent, provoking. "Of course," she answered automatically, "next to Dane, he's the most dependable person I know." The inference that Zach wasn't was clear, and she knew he hadn't missed it.

"Do you really think he'd name me to this position if he thought I couldn't handle it?"

Dara released a deep breath. "I've thought about that, Zach. But I don't think Jarrett has a full understanding of the sort of obstacles these kids face. I know he trusts you, and he probably knew you'd help him out on this, but—"

"No buts, Dara. I'm willing to do this, I *want* to do this. Not just for Jarrett, but because it's a damn good cause and I'm a damn good outfitter. Whatever you think about me personally doesn't matter. What matters is getting these kids the trip they wished for, right?"

Sensing he was leading her into a trap, but unable to see it, she nodded slowly. "Right. But you need my approval to get the board's approval, and you don't have it."

The sober expression on his face broke slowly into a wicked smile. "Yet."

One word, so softly spoken, and the air between them vibrated. With challenge, she told herself. As it always had been between them; Zach challenging her, prodding her until she lost her temper only to find out he'd intentionally staged it to happen at the very worst time—for her.

She pulled up another memory—recalling the time he'd humiliated her in front of Mr. Jackson's biology class by daring her to kiss a frog—which she'd had to take him up on—then showing the rest of the class that the poor thing was dead. The frog had croaked, he'd announced loudly, rather than become a prince for skinny little Dart. Of course, Mr. Jackson had walked in at the exact moment she'd dumped a beakerful of formaldehyde down Zach's shirt.

But this time dredging up old memories didn't work, the tension between them was not as easily relegated to the past.

"What exactly are you proposing?" she asked.

He leaned a jean-clad hip on her desk, and picked up her crystal globe paperweight, bouncing it from palm to palm as if it were blown glass. "What I propose is that I plan a trip for the kids. Then, to ensure it's safe and completely meets the foundation's standards, I will take you out for a trial run so you can personally endorse the setup. My company will absorb the cost of the trial run."

He placed the paperweight gently back on the desk and, bracing his weight on one arm, leaned closer to her. Dara swore she could hear the trapdoor clang shut behind her.

"And, if you don't fully approve," he went on, the gentle tone at complete odds with the victorious gleam in his eyes, "I will fund another trip with the outfitter of your choice. And when Jarrett returns, I'll have him okay his donation for another wish on your list. Fair deal?"

It was beyond fair. It was the perfect solution. No matter how it turned out, the foundation—and more importantly, the kids—prospered. It was a win-win situation. There was absolutely no reason for her to say no.

She nodded slowly. "Deal."

So why did she feel like she'd just kissed a dead frog?

Zach's big, rough hand swallowed hers, but instead of shaking it, he just held it. As Dara stared up at him, ignoring as best she could the warm sensation that was tingling its way up her arm and around the back of her neck, his cocky, triumphant smile faded to something more . . . personal.

In the short time he'd been in her office, he'd revealed more sides than she'd ever expected him to have. And there wasn't one of them that wasn't dangerous to her peace of mind. A peace she'd struggled to achieve.

"I never thought I'd say this," he said quietly, "but it's really good to see you again, Dart."

"Funny, I didn't get that impression about two minutes ago." She'd tried for flippant humor, but winced inwardly when the words came out sounding far too sincere.

"You're just doing your job." The smile turned teasing. "I think I'd have been disappointed if I'd discovered you'd gone completely soft and wishy-washy on me."

Dara felt heat stain her cheeks as he echoed her earlier wish. "Yeah, well, someone's got to keep guys like you in line."

Zach chuckled. "Remind me never to introduce you to Beaudine."

He was making it temptingly easy to relax and enjoy

his company. Which was probably exactly what he was hoping for. As casually as possible, she withdrew her hand from his.

"The kids are lucky to have you on their side, Dara."

Clearing the sudden tightness constricting her throat, she slid her chair back and stood. "Thank you." She'd intended to politely return his earlier platitude about it being nice to see him again, but somehow she suspected that right now, the admission would come out sounding entirely too heartfelt. "Um, the case histories for each of the children are down in the file room. If you'll follow me, I'll get copies for you."

Zach watched Dara scoot from behind her desk and grab a navy blue Dream Foundation blazer from the brass coatrack in the corner. He caught her eye as she slid her arm in one sleeve. His wink just came naturally. As did her responding blush.

Damn if she wasn't still fun to tease. His smile broadened as she shifted her back to him and tugged on the other sleeve. Why *had* he provoked her so often way back then? He'd never really thought about it. As an adolescent boy, it had just seemed natural. Five minutes around her and the next thing he knew she was socking his lights out. Usually with good reason, he admitted with a silent laugh. And yet, as the years passed, he'd never once thought to stop.

Maybe it was because she'd been such a good adversary. Maybe it was because he couldn't charm her like he had everyone else.

He watched her surreptitiously tug the lapels closer in an unsuccessful attempt to hide the coffee stain he'd had a hell of a time keeping his eyes off.

And maybe it was because as a boy, he hadn't known what else to do with a girl that intrigued him like she had. His wide grin was unabashed. Well, he'd learned a lot since then.

He knew exactly what to do with her now.

TWO

The attraction between them—and Zach recognized the signs well enough to know the sizzle in the air was not one-sided—was a surprise. He didn't know what he'd expected to feel on seeing her again, but he knew this wasn't it.

He wondered why Dane had never mentioned that the girl Zach remembered as being more dragon than potential musketeer, still had all that fire. She'd managed to harness it well. But he hadn't a clue why she kept it so carefully concealed behind steady hazel eyes and that firm, business-only mouth.

Zach wasn't fooled. As a child, those chameleon eyes had blazed green when she was angry. And all her cool poise aside, he imagined they still did. Which naturally led him to wonder what else besides anger provoked that intriguing change.

And as for her mouth . . .

Well, his thoughts on what sort of business he'd like to conduct on those lips is what had kept his gaze fastened firmly on that blouse. Which hadn't proved any less provocative.

Dara shifted so as not to brush against him as she walked to the door. Zach was so surprised at the sudden restraint he'd had to use to keep from reaching for her, he didn't move at all. The impulse had been instinctive, as if he touched her so often, the action was natural to him. As if he had the right.

"Zach?"

Her voice broke his train of thought, and he turned to her, the smile on his face not nearly as easy or natural as the one before. He had the odd feeling he'd been transported back to the playground, only one of an adult variety. He closed the distance between them. Of course, now there was no monitor to send him to the principal's office if he misbehaved.

Dara purposely moved back to let him pass through the open door first.

Then again, he thought as he watched her mouth settle into that flat no-nonsense line, she probably still packed a mean left hook.

He stepped past her, fully intending to continue into the hallway and put some much needed space between them. But just as he felt her move in behind him, he found himself turning back to her, trapping her in the intimate space between the door frame—and his frame.

"Dara?" he asked quietly, having no idea what he was going to say.

Dara was too surprised by Zach's sudden move to react, but the familiar way he said her name garnered more of a reaction than she knew what to do with.

Defensive and turned on all at the same time. And she didn't thank him for either feeling. Squaring her shoulders, she looked up at him. "Yes?"

He paused for the longest moment, staring at her in a way that made her discomfort grow. She resisted the urge to squirm.

"You've really changed, you know? And I guess I couldn't help but wonder . . ."

Wary now, she frowned. "Wonder what?"

Bracing an arm on the frame over her head, he leaned closer. "You never struck me as the wand-carrying sort. So how did you get into this line of work? Granting other people's wishes, I mean?"

She was honestly surprised by the question, especially since she'd been expecting something more . . . what? More personal, more intimate maybe? Yeah, right. So he's all grown up and gorgeous as sin with a voice that could seduce the habit off a nun. So what if she was finally old enough to appreciate it? She'd sworn off that potent combination years ago.

Stability. Maturity. Those were the qualities she was attracted to now. The same ones she'd so carefully culti-vated in herself.

She glanced into his eyes. The question had been asked in all sincerity, but the teasing twinkle she found there reminded her that letting her guard down with him had always been dangerous. And despite the hard-won cool control that had elevated her quickly through the executive ranks at the foundation, she knew that with Zach, she was still—and probably always would be—playing out of her league.

"It's a long story, Zach," she said, trying to edge her way past him.

His slight shift blocked her escape. "I didn't ask out of idle curiosity. I really want to know. What happened to that little girl who was willing to slay dragons with her bare hands in order to be D'Artagnan?"

Oh, he was dangerous all right. After a fifteen-year absence from her life and a shared past that wasn't exactly harmonious, he'd taken less than thirty minutes to mount a more effective assault on her well-built defenses than any man she'd met since Daniel had died over eight years ago.

Dara knew just how easy he'd make it for her to break down and share with him the parts of her past that had so largely shaped who she'd become. Just as she knew where that would lead. And she'd be right back in the place she'd busted her backside and most of her soul to get away from.

"We really should get those files so you can look them over before the board meeting," she said quickly, catching that determined look in his eyes and wanting to end this before he could speak again.

But he didn't step back, or let her pass. Instead he leaned closer, close enough that she could feel the heat of his body, close enough so that her gaze could naturally follow the strong column of his neck until it gave way to the stubble that shaded his jaw. Close enough that she couldn't help but notice how his lower lip was just slightly fuller than his upper one. Close enough so that if he parted them slightly and she shifted forward even the tiniest bit, she could—

Whatever she might have thought or, heaven forbid, done next, was instantly erased by the sound of someone clearing his throat.

Dara closed her eyes and willed herself to melt for real—right through the floor. Zach had done it again. Straightening, she called on every bit of self-control and poise she could muster and ducked beneath his arm.

Sure enough, Old Man Cavendish was standing not two feet behind Zach, a very disapproving frown on his face. Not that she'd ever seen him look any differently, but this time *she* was the reason for it.

"Mr. Cavendish," she said brightly, hoping her smile didn't look as fake as it felt. "Is there something I can do for you?"

The thin, elderly man looked down at her with narrowed black eyes set deeply beneath bushy gray eyebrows. She happened to catch Zach's eye at that exact moment. He flashed a quick wink and a knowing smile that made her suddenly want to laugh. Hard. Horrified at the sound threatening to bubble from her throat, she quickly covered it with a cough, making absolutely certain not to look at Zach again.

Ten minutes with Zach Brogan and it was like the principal's office all over again.

"What you can do, young lady," Mr. Cavendish said in his perfectly enunciated dictatorial tone, "is keep your personal business on personal time. We're understaffed and overworked as it is. I'm sure you have something on your desk requiring your attention." He let his censorious gaze roam up and down Zach's large frame, obviously not in the least impressed. Then, with the dignified bearing more suitable to a man who ruled nations than one who ran a charitable foundation, he turned and walked away.

The instant his tall, bony frame disappeared around the corner at the far end of the hall, Dara rounded on Zach. "I'll thank you never to put me in that position again!"

Zach grinned and placed his hands on his hips, mocking her indignant stance. "Most certainly, madam." Then he relaxed and leaned toward her, his voice lowered to a rough whisper. "Just tell me what position you prefer. I aim to please."

I'll just bet you do, she thought darkly. Not daring to say another word, she turned and marched down the hall.

Zach caught up to her as she turned the corner and swiftly moved in front of her, blocking her path. She tried to go around him, but he shifted and blocked her again.

"Haven't you played enough sophomoric games for today?" She raised her hand in defeat at his smile. "Never mind. Stupid question."

"I wasn't playing games, Dara. I'm sorry your boss is such an old prune, but you have to admit—"

"If you were so sorry, why didn't you say something?"

"Because," he answered immediately, "you don't strike me as the kind of woman who'd appreciate interference when it comes to doing her job."

He had her there. Damn. How dare he get all perceptive on her just when she had the upper hand? "You're right. I can handle Mr. Cavendish."

Zach grinned and moved next to her as she determinedly stepped around him and continued down the hallway. When he remained silent, Dara breathed a small sigh of relief. She'd never had her emotions so jumbled up so quickly, or so often, and she relished the chance to get herself back on track.

She stopped in front of a large oak-paneled door and reached for the knob. Before she could swing it open, Zach leaned down and whispered in her ear.

"But I have to know, were those eyebrows of his real?"

The laughter she'd repressed earlier burst out without warning at the same instant she opened the door. The sound died on a choked gurgle as the ongoing conversation inside the room fell into a hushed silence and the silver-haired heads of ten distinguished men sitting around the large boardroom table swiveled as one in her direction.

"Is there a problem, Miss Colbourne?" the man at the head of the table inquired.

She swallowed hard and offered the gentleman, who just happened to be the head of Dream Foundation's board of trustees, a weak smile. "No, sir, not at all. I'm sorry to have interrupted." Dara quietly backed out of the room and softly clicked the door shut, then groaned to herself. That made twice in less than five minutes.

She was going to kill him.

She whirled to find Zach holding open the door several feet farther down the hallway. "Is this the room you were looking for?" he inquired with all the innocence of a choirboy.

Fighting a smile, she walked past him into the file room. "Yes, thank you."

By the time the door shut behind her, she was half-way down the aisle between the tall rows of file cabinets.

A shadow fell over her as she pulled a drawer open, followed by his warm breath on her neck.

"I'm curious," he said, his voice impossibly deep. "While you've been busy playing fairy godmother, has anyone . . . you know, changed your pumpkin into a carriage?"

Zach watched with increased interest as Dara's shoulders tensed, the fine line of her neck straightened slightly. He curled his hands into fists to keep from touching her. She was easy to tease, quick on the defensive, and she still gave as good as she got. She was also fighting tooth and nail to hide her response to him. Zach was totally captivated.

He should care that his reaction to her was far more intense than he ever expected, but he didn't. Fifteen minutes with her was equal to the high he got climbing the wall of an ice glacier. Or, more aptly in her case, a dangerous descent into a still-active volcano.

He knew. He'd done both. But Dara Colbourne was simply an adventure unto herself. The appeal of which he didn't entirely understand, but was finding almost impossible to ignore.

"If you're asking whether I'm seeing someone, the answer is, it's none of your business," she said, without turning.

He grinned. Damn, but he was enjoying this. "Just wanted to make sure that when I take you up on that mountain, I'm not sending inappropriate signals to someone."

The file drawer snapped shut with a solid thwack. She spun around and plastered the files against his chest.

"First of all," she said, her hazel eyes turning a very intoxicating shade of green, "if there *was* someone to send inappropriate signals to, he would trust me implicitly, so there would be no need for your concern." She ducked neatly under his arm and marched to the door. With one hand on the doorknob, she pivoted back to face him. "And secondly, you are assuming quite a bit if you think you've got this job in the bag. I'll expect a full report on every detail of the weekend trip before I decide whether to go with you or not."

Zach closed the distance between them in three easy strides. Chin tipped up, brown hair dancing in soft waves around her small face, eyes blazing, and back ramrod straight. He took in every detail, unsure what it was about her that had him more turned on than he could ever recall being. And he'd had a lot more provocation from a number of far more willing partners.

Maybe it was the coffee stain peeking out from behind the lapel of her genderless foundation blazer; maybe it was seeing those irises change color again and knowing he was the one responsible for it; maybe it was the whitened knuckles of her fist gripping the doorknob that announced she was far less composed than she'd like him to believe.

And maybe it was some genetic predetermination that mandated he couldn't be around Dara Colbourne for any length of time without finding his control completely pushed to the limit. Only the limits he was pushing as a man had entirely different consequences than those he'd pushed as a boy.

Whatever it was, it was damn exciting. And challenging. And he'd never been one to walk away from a challenge.

He braced his hand on the door above her head and leaned in close, unable to keep from pushing, testing. From discovering for himself where the margin of safety ended and the temptations of risk began.

"You'll go up that mountain with me, Dara. And you'll approve the trip." Her lips parted as if she were about to speak, but Zach proceeded, his body tightening, recognizing and enjoying the thrill of walking the fine line between safety and danger. "And you'll have the best damn time of your life doing it too. That's a Brogan guarantee."

She took an audible breath, her chest brushing ever so slightly against his. Feeling a distinct wobble in the high wire he was balancing on, Zach knew it was time to pull back. Past time. He laid his hand on hers, turned the knob and pulled the door open.

She tugged her hand from beneath his, but he instinctively caught it and curled his fingers over hers, enclosing her fist in his.

Her skin was soft, her fingers strong. He rubbed his fingertips lightly over the pulse on her inner wrist. The rapid pulse. He grinned. "It was good seeing you again, Dart. Call me after the board meeting."

He shot her a wink, then laughed as she yanked her hand away, the tempest in her eyes warning him to retreat for the day before he was nursing a black eye. Or worse.

He was whistling as he approached his truck, breaking into a smile as he eyed the words slashed in vivid red along the shiny black side of his pickup. *Born To Be Wild*.

"Some days more than others," he said, then chuckled as he climbed into the cab, the fatigue from his thirty-six-hour trek from Chile to Virginia suddenly a distant, nonexistent concern. He slapped the folders down on the seat, dug out his Steppenwolf cassette and punched it in the tape deck as he revved the engine. Oh yeah, seeing Dara Colbourne again had been mighty fine indeed.

"Yes," Zach repeated into the phone the following afternoon, "that's exactly what I want. Four big wheels, good on average to mildly rough terrain, average inclines, completely hand operable."

Zach doodled another parachute in the margin of the yellow legal pad, his attention only half on the conversation. The other half was wondering how Scotty and Cortinez were doing in Chile while he sat in the stifling confines of the office in his house. He spent more time planning trips now than running them, but the ones he did take on personally he hated like hell to miss.

"Good," he said a few moments later, "that sounds fine. I'll be out on Thursday to look at it. Thanks, Frank, I really appreciate you doing this on such short notice."

Zach hung up the phone just as Beaudine strode into the room. Her silver-white hair was caught up in a tight bun covered with a net—deep purple today, the exact shade of the slogan scrawled across the white apron she wore over her sleek black nylon jogging suit. It read: Cajuns Give Deep South A Whole New Meaning.

He smiled, not caring that his slumped position gave away just how tired he was. He nodded at her attire. "Does this mean you finally asked Frank for a date?" Yesterday her apron had read: Kiss Me or Die a Slow Painful Death.

The only reply he got was a snort.

His grin broadened. "At least you've stopped playing hard to get."

"Hard to get!" She slapped a small stack of folders on his desk, and set a tall glass of iced tea next to them. *"Bon Dieu, cher,* but I'm about as easy to get as today's paper." Without a break in movement, she scooped up the small plastic pitcher she'd left on her last pass through and watered the plants lining the windowsill. "The Fujimora deal is there." She nodded at the manila folders. "Montague will call next week to set up the helicopter thing. And you have two faxes coming in later this afternoon with quotes from the Nepalese and Tibetans on the permits for that Himalayan trip. Drink your tea, *cher.*"

"Did Frank say yes or no?" was Zach's only response.

The plants done, Beaudine whipped a dust rag from the deep pocket of her apron. Tackling the closest bookshelf, she roughly wiped the dust from the surface. "That man, what he doesn't know would fill the Bayou Teche, don't I know." Her grumbled curses quickly slipped into her native Cajun dialect.

"What was that?" Zach prodded, unable to resist. "You wouldn't be casting some old voodoo spell on Frank, now would you, *chère?"*

"And it's not like I'd give this body to just any ol' coot, I tell you what!" She straightened the rolled-up maps that filled the antique umbrella stand in the corner. "And that ol' coot knows it. If he thinks I have time to wait for him to get around to making the first move . . . At this rate I could be dead a year before I get his clothes off."

Laughing in earnest now, Zach held up his hand. "Enough, enough. I don't think I want to know any more." He let her settle down a moment, before asking, "She here yet?"

"Mais non, cher. She called on the other line a few minutes ago and said she was stuck behind some accident on 29. She'll be here soon." Beaudine walked over to the fern hanging from the ceiling behind Zach, knocking his feet off his desk to the floor as she passed.

She deftly snapped the dead fronds from the bushy plant. "You too tired to sit straight? You go to bed early." She aimed a disparaging look at the floor and the desk that were littered with chunks of dried red clay from his heavy hiking boots. "Dusting is one thing, *cher*, but I draw the line at lifting the vacuum cleaner onto the desk."

"Ah, an ol' gator wrassler like you?" he shot back. "You could tilt this big wooden desk over with one hand and be done with it. You don't fool me."

"Don't tempt me." She rattled the back of his chair as she passed by, making Zach grab the edge of his desk to keep from falling over backward. She was tall, lean, and faster in her Reeboks than a woman her age had any right being. Although exactly what age that was he had never determined. In the six years she'd worked for him, he'd narrowed it down to somewhere between sixty-five and eighty.

The swishing sound of nylon stopped abruptly as she turned in the doorway. "And the only fool I see is you. Why you making Miz Colbourne drive all the way out here when she's so busy is none of my business, but if you ask me—"

"Dara dragged me all the way home from Chile." Zach tilted his chair back again, smiling at Beaudine's scowl. "She can drive as far as Field's Corner. Besides, she probably hasn't been back to Madison County in ages." Knowing he would never win the battle but loving the challenge nonetheless, he adopted a dead-on Cajun accent and added, "And someone who works as hard as Miz Colbourne deserves a nice quiet afternoon in the country, don't you think, *ma pichouette*?"

Beaudine's mumbled, "Little girl, my—" degenerated into Cajun swearing that had him laughing again as she left.

Zach propped his feet back on the desk and returned his attention to the legal pad in his hands.

He sighed deeply, absently rubbing at a tight spot in his chest as he went over the notes he'd made on each of the four children scheduled for the trip.

Teddy, age ten, paraplegic, wheelchair bound, had use of arms, hands, and neck. Brandon, age nine, advanced case of multiple sclerosis, also wheelchair bound, limited coordination of arms and hands. Jonas, age nine, muscular dystrophy, leg braces on both legs, but could walk with crutches and had full function of his arms and hands. Andie . . .

Andie. Zach closed his eyes and rubbed his thumbs across his eyelids, not having to look at his notes to know what they said. Andie, age ten. Cancer. Wheelchair bound. Frail, but full use of her arms and hands. Probably wouldn't see age twelve.

"Damn," he whispered, the grittiness behind his closed eyes not entirely from lack of sleep. He massaged the back of his neck, doing little to ease the tension that had knotted there. He'd read the case histories last night before turning in, and the details had haunted him since. Life's inequities and the strength these kids had to have in order to face them day in and day out was sobering. Combined with the potent memory of those hazel-green eyes flashing at him, demanding that he let someone more qualified handle the job, had all but robbed him of any chance at sleep.

At some point, in the quiet hours long past midnight, he'd made a solemn vow to himself. Two, actually. One: To plan the most incredible trip for those kids he had within his power to give. And two: To pursue whatever it was that he'd felt with Dara.

Because, as Dara had observed and as those four kids understood on the most intimate level, life was just too damn short to waste wondering about what could have been.

The sound of gravel beneath tires jerked him from his thoughts. Beaudine's congenial greeting of "How y'all are," at the front door echoed down the hallway to his office. He listened to Dara return the hello, then go on to politely assure Beaudine she was fine, really, and no she wasn't thirsty or hungry and that she was sure she could find the office all by herself and please not to go to any trouble on her account.

Zach glanced at the clock on the wall. Less than twenty seconds. Not bad. A world record for first-timers.

The clicking of heels grew louder as Dara approached. He was only vaguely surprised to feel his muscles, his entire body in fact, tighten in anticipation. The sensation was similar to the feeling the instant before jumping from a plane, or off a cliff.

He leaned back deeper in the chair and savored it.

Dara's light rap on the door frame commanded and received his full attention. "Sorry I'm late." She entered the room with a rustle of soft fabric and an even softer scent of perfume. She wore a muted red blazer over a jet-black skirt—a skirt that showed more leg than he thought someone as short as Dara could possibly have. And another pure white blouse, buttoned tightly at the neck and softened with a bow. Tasteful, understated, businesslike. He wondered if she realized it was still sexy as hell.

"I can't believe I'm in this house again." She smiled as she glanced around. "I haven't been back in this area since I was a teenager. I forgot how beautiful the Shenandoahs were." Her attention was on everything but him. "I see you've turned your dad's old study into an office."

Her gaze strayed from the jam-packed floor-to-ceiling bookshelves covering two walls, to the multitude of overlapping maps thumbtacked all over the other two walls, to the clumps of red clay littering the top of his cluttered desk. "Of sorts," she added wryly.

Zach's chest tightened a notch, and his smile wasn't as smooth as he would have liked. How did she manage that? He actually found himself resisting the urge to sit up straight and take his feet off his desk. It was a bit late for making a good first impression.

"Have a seat," he said, motioning toward the chair on the other side of his desk.

She did. "I see you've gone over the case files." She nodded toward the folders spread on his desk.

He started to speak, but she chose that moment to cross her legs, and all that came out was a mumbled noise he hoped she took for a yes. He was forced to lift his boots from the desk as the sudden need to find a more comfortable position overruled his determination not to let her dictate his behavior.

"I've already made a few preliminary calls to some friends of mine," he began.

"Friends?"

He looked up. The smile came easier this time. "I do have some, you know."

"Imagine that." The lift at the corners of her mouth softened the sarcasm in her response. "What exactly do these friends have to do with the camping trip?"

"Well, after looking over the background and medical reports, I realized the most obvious problem we have is overcoming their limited mobility. I've got someone working on an idea I had to help fix that."

"When I called to tell you that the board liked your idea Friday afternoon, I did make clear that until you're fully approved, any expense you incur—"

Zach held up his hand. "I know. Don't worry about it." He shrugged. "After all, it's only money." Her frown was disapproving, as he'd known it would be. Oh yeah, it was obvious she thought the world of him.

"So," he continued doing his damnedest to ignore the need to shift in his seat again, "do you want to hear my ideas?"

THREE

Dara gazed steadily at Zach. Even clean-shaven he still looked rugged. When she'd first arrived, he'd appeared a bit weary, as if he hadn't slept much, either. Looking at him now, she questioned her earlier judgment. His deep brown eyes were animated, and his handsome features were relaxed and totally open to her. She'd already marked off this afternoon's trip as a major waste of her time—a power play on his part she'd decided not to challenge. But his obvious enthusiasm for the project—one she still had no intention of letting him run—was nonetheless infectious.

Funny, she'd never been susceptible before.

Adopting what she considered a healthy amount of wariness, she uncrossed her legs and leaned forward in order to see what he'd written. "Nice parachutes," she said, motioning to the numerous doodles on the page. "But I doubt the children's parents would be receptive to you dropping them from planes onto the mountaintop."

His laughter was rich, warm, and entirely too appealing. "And here I thought I'd come up with such a brilliant plan. I guess you win." He affected a wounded sigh. "And I was so hoping you'd love the idea."

Dara laughed despite her best attempt not to.

"Actually," he continued, "since three of the four kids are in wheelchairs, and the other one has leg braces and uses crutches, I figured I'd better find alternative transportation or backpack the kids up with the rest of the supplies."

"So what did you have in mind?"

"A buddy of mine is going to reconfigure a few buggies, sort of like All-Terrain Vehicles. Make them hand operable."

"You plan to put them in ATV's? Zach, those things are unstable at best, and very dangerous at worst!"

This was exactly the sort of irresponsible thinking she'd expected from him. Exactly the sort of proof she needed to get him off the assignment before actually having to go up the mountain with him.

Which didn't come close to explaining why her moment of triumph felt a whole lot more like disappointment.

"I said Frank was modifying them. Bigger, softer tires, slower speed and completely hand-controlled." He leaned back in the chair. "Of course, if they get real good with them going uphill, I figured we could race back down."

"Zach!"

"You're so easy." His smile was sexy and teasing as he stood and walked around the desk, leaning one hip on the corner. "I was kidding about the race."

Dara lifted an eyebrow, and he laughed.

"Okay, so maybe I thought a few races—on flat ground—would be fun. Kids race in wheelchairs all the time." He raised his hands in a conciliatory gesture. "But I'll let you make the call."

"I don't know about this, Zach."

"So come with me to Frank's place on Thursday and see for yourself."

Ah, the trap had been sprung, and she hadn't even seen it coming. With an inward sigh, she didn't bother to contemplate arguing. If they were going up that mountain together—and that was still a big "if" in her mind—then she'd be less than responsible if she didn't check out all aspects of his plans beforehand. Besides, if these souped-up ATV's didn't meet her standards, then the whole thing could be over in less than forty-eight hours. She'd already compiled a list of well-reputed family camping outfitters and could have one signed on as early as Friday.

"I'll have to check my schedule."

"No problem," he replied easily. "I know you're busy. So is Frank. I told him we'd be there about six."

"He's expecting me, is he? The ego has grown in proportion to the body."

"Actually, I think the body just caught up to it over the years." His grin was totally unrepentant. "But it was your ego I was banking on. No way would you let me go ahead with this without checking out every little detail yourself."

"Touché," she admitted with a reluctant smile.

He lifted a hand, and she took it without thinking as he pulled her up. Only he didn't let go, and she found herself a half step away from standing between his parted knees.

"Frank's garage is in Leesburg. You want to meet me there?" His voice was soft and smooth.

"Sure." She gently tugged her hand from his. He let his fingertips trail across her palm, the wide pads rough and warm against her skin. "I'll, uh . . ." Her gaze had fallen to his hand on hers, but when she lifted it back to his eyes, the words had just died in her throat.

His eyes were so . . . brown. No golden flecks, no hint of any light. Just rich, dark brown. She watched with an absent sort of fascination as his pupils dilated.

"Dart?" His tone somehow imbued the silly childhood nickname with more than a little adult interest.

"Yes?" Her voice was barely more than a whisper.

"You want directions?"

"Directions?" For some reason her brain refused to compute that response. She felt her neck and ears heat. "Ah, yes, of course," she said, as she took a small step away from him. Carefully avoiding his face, she unzipped her Day-Timer and slipped the slender pen from its holder. "I can get to Leesburg, just give me an address."

"Frank's place is on Catoctin Circle, about halfway."

She scribbled that down, suddenly wanting—needing —to be out of there, away from him. "Do you have his number? In case something comes up?"

Zach slid the pen from her fingertips and carefully tucked it back under the thin leather band. "If something comes up, call me, not Frank." He smiled. "If I'm not here, Beaudine'll know how to reach me."

Dara found herself holding her breath and forced it

out slowly, then swallowed to moisten her suddenly dry throat. She quietly zipped the case shut. "Fine."

She walked to the door, knowing she should simply keep on moving until she was in her car and driving away. But some little voice in her head had to break the silence, had to ease the tension that had again sprung up between them. A tension completely foreign to any sort she'd experienced with him as a child. For that matter, except for yesterday in her office, she'd never felt it as an adult, either. Not even with Daniel.

And it was a tension she wasn't entirely sure she didn't like. But she *was* sure she shouldn't.

Which was why she turned in the doorway and said, "Getting the children up the mountain is only part of it, Brogan. You still have to plan three entire days. And ATV's aren't the solution to everything."

"Don't worry, Dara." His grin made a shambles of her attempt to keep it all business between them. "I know this is only the beginning."

Dara pulled into Frank's parking lot two days later, noticing right off the unusually neat and orderly appearance of the garage. There were several other cars parked along the edge of the lot next to the larger of the two buildings. And a black pickup she recognized from her trip to Zach's house. The cherry-red slogan on the side removed any doubt as to its owner.

Born To Be Wild. She shook her head in disgust even as she smiled. That said it in a nutshell.

Next to the garage was a small white building that

appeared to be the office. She parked next to Zach's truck and headed in that direction.

Zach startled her when he stepped from the shadows of the open bay door. He motioned her inside. "This way."

Hello to you, too, she almost said, but stopped herself in time. Business, she reminded herself, as she had several times over the last two days and another dozen times in the car on the way there. Strictly business.

Just because he filled out faded jeans better than a cigarette-ad cowboy and a T-shirt better than the latest martial arts hero was no reason she couldn't conduct herself like an adult.

Unfortunately, just watching him walk in front of her was making her feel exceedingly . . . adult.

"Where's Frank?" she asked abruptly, so annoyed at her preoccupation with Zach that she barely shifted in time to avoid brushing against a rolling tool cart, the row of drawers half open and filled with grimy equipment.

"Right here," called a gravelly voice. A moment later a man in a wheelchair rolled into view from behind a car jacked a few feet off the ground. His wiry frame was garbed in traditional grease-covered overalls, his thinning gray hair putting him at his mid-sixties in her estimation.

Suddenly it clicked in her mind what it was about the garage that had seemed out of place. It wasn't the orderliness—it was the arrangement. Her gaze darted quickly to the walls. The tools and various belts and such were all hanging no higher than four feet from the ground.

She didn't dare look at Zach as she shook the hand

Frank had just wiped clean and stretched out to her. "I'm pleased to meet you," she said sincerely.

"Mutual," he grunted. "The go-carts are back here." Frank spun the wheelchair around and headed for an open door leading to a small lot behind the garage.

"Go-carts?" she whispered to Zach, alarm creeping into her voice.

"That's what Frank calls them. Don't worry, you'll see." He stepped aside and let her pass through the door first.

There on the back lot were two small, four-wheeled vehicles, neither even close to being new if the dents and patches of missing paint were any indication.

Frank rolled over to the nearest one. "I know they aren't pretty, but they'll do the job right enough." He shifted back a few feet and motioned with his hand. "Go ahead, hop in."

"Me?" Dara turned uncertainly to Zach.

"Of course you," Zach replied. "You're the one who needs to approve them." He grasped her elbow and propelled her forward a few steps. "Besides"—he grinned unabashedly—"I already tried one out. Too slow for my taste, but these days I guess they'll be right up your alley."

Dara didn't bother answering him. There was nothing wrong with slow and sedate. But she wasn't going to let him bait her into an argument about their opposing lifestyle choices. She spared a quick glance at her silk dress and low heels, wondering why she hadn't counted on this possibility.

She caught the knowing twinkle in Zach's eyes, and some tiny remaining seed of her childhood sprang forth in response. Before she had time to question it, Dara had plopped her Day-Timer on the ground, hitched up her skirt well above her knees and stepped into the recessed well between the front wheels. The seat had been modified to a bucket-type contraption so the driver didn't have to straddle it.

She settled in, the area a bit small even for her, making her wonder how in the world Zach had tried the thing. She didn't ask. "Sort of reminds me of a mini dune buggy."

Frank leaned over and pointed to the buttons on the left side of the dashboard and the two small levers by her left knee. "I simplified as much as possible. The key unlocks the ignition. Once it's in, turn it to the left. Then all they need to do is push the green button to start it up."

"I see. And I guess the red button stops it."

"That shuts the engine off. The brake is the bottom padded area in the center of the steering wheel. The top one is the horn."

"What about the levers?"

"The one with the black knob is the emergency brake, the one with the yellow knob is to put it in reverse. The speed is controlled by the pressure pads lining the steering wheel." He motioned to the black rubber strips on the sides of the small wheel. "Just give them a little pressure and off you go. Top speed is about five miles per hour. Zach told me the kids were nine and ten years old. If they can handle motorized wheelchairs, they can handle this."

She started to speak, but Zach cut in. "I know Brandon's coordination is limited. Frank will attach a coupling device to each car so they can be linked together if necessary."

Dara smiled, truly impressed. Turning to Frank, she said, "This is wonderful. Can I really try it?" She glanced up and caught Zach looking at her, obviously pleased by her acceptance of Frank's hard work. Well, there was no point in denying it. "Okay, Brogan, you win this round." Then she gave a little whoop, pressed the green button and putted forward. "Not exactly a bucking bronc of a ride," she said as she turned smoothly at the edge of the lot, "but it seems perfect for the kids."

She drove around the back lot twice, checking out the reverse speed before pulling back in between Zach and Frank.

"I'll connect a shoulder and chest harness to the back of the seat," Frank added, "and they should wear helmets, but otherwise this is as good as it gets."

"And it'll do okay on the hills? Even downhill?"

"They may have to work the brake coming back down, but it shouldn't be difficult since it stays in such a low gear."

Zach appeared at her side to help her climb out. "I plan to keep them on as level a grade as possible," he said, "so there won't be any steep climbs or descents. It will take a bit longer that way, but getting there is half the fun. Right?"

Dara took his hand, knowing it would have been a less than graceful exit without his help. His hand lingered an extra instant or two before dropping away, the caress of his fingers up her wrist and across her inner elbow so slight, she thought she might have imagined it. A quick glance at Zach's brown eyes told her she hadn't.

Doing her best to ignore him, she turned to Frank. "This is really incredible after only two days." She looked over her shoulder and added, "The kids' parents will have to approve them, of course. But I admit, I am impressed." She turned back to Frank. "Have you done this sort of thing before?"

He nodded. "I work with a few of the local handicap groups, and I've done a few things for the Special Olympics people in the area." He tapped the chrome sides of his wheelchair. "I was a mechanic long before I ended up in this thing, so it was only natural to want to tinker with them, see if I could adapt them."

Dara suspected it went deeper than his casual explanation, but didn't push it. "Well, I think it's wonderful. Will you be able to use these again . . . later?" She almost said after the trip, but Zach had already scored one big win today, so it wasn't a wise idea to let him think he had it sewn up. He didn't, not by a long shot.

Frank squinted against the sun as he looked up at Zach. "All depends, I guess." Not bothering to explain the cryptic remark, he wheeled around and headed back to the garage. "I'll get the other two done and store 'em inside at night. Just let me know when you're gonna come for 'em."

"Will do," Zach called after him. "Thanks again, Frank, I'll call you later. I owe you a big one."

"Yeah, I'll bill you." The older man's laugh was more a rough bark and faded as he disappeared inside.

Dara turned to Zach, the question out before she had time to think about it. "Didn't you pay the man for all this?"

Zach took her elbow in his big hand and steered her

around the outside of the building. "Frank's taken care of."

Dara opened her mouth to ask exactly what he meant by that but snapped it shut again. After all, it was none of her business. Another indication of Zach's casual "don't worry, be happy" lifestyle, no doubt.

Just the same, she made a mental note to contact Frank on her own later and find out if he'd be receptive to the foundation throwing some work his way. Off the top of her head she knew at least a dozen parents who'd be interested in having Frank do some modification work for their wheelchair-bound children.

"How about a bite to eat?" Zach asked as they walked toward her sedate blue compact. "There's a great steak house just down the street."

Dara casually lifted her elbow from the tingling warmth of his light grasp and fished for her keys. "This went more quickly than I'd anticipated. I really should get back to the office. I have a ton of work I could make a dent in."

"But you hadn't planned on going back."

"No." She smiled, her expression one of determination, knowing where he was heading this time. "But now I am. I appreciate your having this set up so nicely for me to check out. Call when you have the rest of the trip outlined and we'll set up a meeting."

She pulled her door open and scooted inside. She stuck the key in the ignition and pushed the button to lower her window, fully prepared to toss him a casual good-bye and zip out of the lot. What she wasn't prepared for was finding his gorgeous face a mere inch away from hers. With the glass lowered, she could feel his breath against her cheek.

"All work and no play," he admonished lightly. "Can't you spare an hour of wand waving to reminisce over old times with a childhood friend?"

"All play and no work, Brogan," she countered. "Someone's got to work. Besides," she added, "I don't really think rehashing our particular past would be advisable while trying to eat. Do you?"

His lips spread slowly into a reckless grin. Dara felt her heart speed up as a tiny trickle of sweat wended its way between her breasts. No doubt just a reaction to sitting in the stifling heat of the car after being all closed up under the hot June sun.

He leaned a bit farther into the window, and it took all her willpower not to shift away from him. Or shift closer.

"You hold a grudge for a long time, Dart," he said. "I'm not a jerky kid anymore. I promise I won't make you kiss, hold, or swallow anything you don't want to."

Dara's eyes widened, and a scarlet flush crept up her neck and across her cheeks. She could only pray fervently that he'd chalk it up to the heat. Because if he ever, *ever* guessed what the immediate images his words had triggered in her mind had been of—

Dear God, she'd simply have to kill herself. It would certainly be less painful and humiliating than listening to Zach laugh himself sick. And then, of course, just for old time's sake, he'd probably feel compelled to share it with Dane and Jarrett. She shuddered.

"You're remembering the time I dared you to eat the

ants, aren't you?" He said it so sincerely, and looked so contrite.

It struck her as more than ironic that Zach was actually exhibiting honest concern—and she was the one with her mind in the gutter. She couldn't help it. She burst out laughing. In fact, she laughed until tears ran down her face, probably taking half of her mascara with it. "Actually, no," she said finally. "I'd forgotten about that one. But thanks for reminding me." Still fighting the giggles, she hiccuped. He must think she was a lunatic. She wasn't too sure about her mental state at the moment either.

Looking confused and more than a little concerned, Zach reached a hand in the car and felt her forehead. "You okay?"

She nodded, and leaned away from the heat of his palm, feeling suddenly vulnerable and a bit foolish. "Fine. I'm fine, really. I don't know what came over me," she lied. "I really should be getting back."

He studied her for another moment, then smiled. "Well, if you won't eat with me, would you mind giving me a lift as far as Dulles? I have a meeting with a client in a couple of hours."

Zach took advantage of Dara's momentary surprise to move around the back of the car—even he didn't dare risk going around the front—and slid into the passenger seat. He also didn't comment when he had to tuck his knees almost under his chin to fit into the bucket seat. In this case, beggars wouldn't dare be choosers.

Dara closed her window and put the car into reverse. "Why are you having a meeting at the airport?"

"Mr. Fujimora will only be in town for twenty-four

hours. So I'm meeting him before his flight out for Tokyo."

Zach almost laughed as he watched her try to hide her curiosity. For whatever reason, as an adult she'd suppressed her true nature. Gone was the daredevil, gone was the girl whose sole purpose in life had been to push herself—and him—to the limit. She'd been so much like her dad. Zach's smile dimmed. Was the crash that killed her father responsible for this turnabout? Zach knew that George Colbourne had been a private pilot and that he'd died when his small jet had gone down during a snowstorm in the Blue Ridge just west of their Madison County home. A snowstorm Mr. Colbourne had known about, but had flown in anyway.

Dara had been eleven when he'd died. And while Zach remembered just how devastated she and Dane had been by their father's death—Dara in particular as she was like a miniature version of her dad in both looks and attitude—he also knew that her wild ways had eventually resurfaced. Certainly before she'd moved away at fifteen.

So what *had* happened? Was it really just as simple as she'd grown up and changed direction? Not that there was anything wrong with her career. He admired the hell out of her for the important work she was doing. But her derogatory comments about his choice of profession—which the girl he'd known would have understood and championed—had him thinking that maybe she was purposely playing life safe. Busying herself slaying other people's dragons so she wouldn't have to face her own.

He watched her carefully, as she turned away to check traffic before pulling out of the lot. They'd reached the corner light when she suddenly stomped on the brake, ignoring the blare of the horn coming from the car behind her. Zach reflexively pressed his hands to the roof of the car to keep from eating his kneecaps.

"Wait a minute, why am I giving you a lift?" she demanded. "I don't even remember saying yes."

"Frank is doing some work on my shocks," he replied calmly.

"And just how did you expect to make your meeting with Mr. Fujimora?" The car behind them laid on the horn again. She shoved the car into first gear and turned onto Route 7. "Never mind. I'm sure wining and dining me into driving you was cheaper than cab fare. And you really lucked out this time. You didn't even have to spring for the food."

"The dinner invite is still open," he said, struggling to pull the narrow seat belt across his chest as Dara darted through traffic.

"No thanks. I'm sure you can grab something at the airport while you wait." She spared a quick glance at him as she rolled to a stop at the next red light. "What sort of trip are you planning this time?"

So she couldn't let it go. Maybe the old Dara was closer to the surface than he'd suspected. He wondered if she suspected. "I can't tell you."

"What do you mean you can't tell me?" she demanded. "You plan vacations—and I use that term loosely—not espionage." Another honk from behind them had her muttering as she roared through the intersection.

Zach wedged his hand between his thigh and the door and gripped the handle. "Actually, this time it's a little of both. But that's all I can tell you. Any more and I'd have to kill you."

"Very funny." Dara glared at him briefly, then returned her attention to the highway as she moved swiftly into the other lane to avoid running up on the fender of the slow-moving van in front of them.

"That is, if you don't kill me first," Zach muttered, letting loose a sigh of relief when the light ahead turned red. Had it been only moments ago that he'd silently accused her of playing life safe? Apparently that didn't apply when she was behind the wheel.

"I heard that, Brogan." Dara looked over at him. "I'll have you know I have a perfect driving record. No tickets, no accidents."

"So, there is a god."

"Ha, ha, ha," she retorted. "For a thrill-seeker, you sure scare easy."

It was like watching an exotic butterfly emerge from a plain brown chrysalis. Had he read her completely wrong? He didn't think so. She made her opinions quite clear. And often.

So what then? Was it his presence that brought out this side of her? He couldn't ignore how incredibly intrigued he was by that idea. Not to mention challenged.

He loved challenges.

"The key to a successful thrill," he stated, recalling her latest slur on his profession, "is planning carefully and thoroughly so you have as much control as the situation allows. The further you reduce the unnecessary risks, the more fully you can appreciate the unavoidable ones.

"Being the passenger in your car," he continued

tightly, as she deftly tucked the compact between two cars in the fast lane without turning a hair, "doesn't remotely fulfill any of those requirements."

"I haven't gone over the speed limit—"

He snorted.

"—by more than a mile or two," she added, obviously enjoying his discomfort, "I used my turn signal every time I changed lanes—"

"I hardly think one blink as you cut back and forth is what the Department of Motor Vehicles handbook had in mind regarding safe lane changes."

"Oh, for heaven's sake," she said. "I'm beginning to think you're nothing but a big fraud."

He had to bite his tongue to keep from making the same accusation. Did she have any idea how beautiful she was all fired up like this? "Fraud?" he shot back. "Take the first exit and go toward the hotel. I'll have you know I've done things that would curl your toes." He lifted his hands then quickly grabbed the dashboard as she pulled into the first parking space and stopped on a dime. "Why am I defending myself to you?"

She turned to face him. "I'm sure I have no idea," she said sweetly. "But I'll admit it's nice to play offense for a change."

Zach stared at her for two long beats. "You're knocking me totally out," he said, breaking into laughter. A second later, she joined him.

The sound slowly faded, though their smiles remained. When Dara's smile faltered, Zach felt his pulse speed up. Her lips parted slightly, and he had to clench his hands to keep from reaching for her. "You sure you can't fit in a quick dinner?" he asked, his voice husky. "I

imagine the Marriott here has a nice dining room."
When she didn't immediately say no, he added, "We can
use the time to go over my other ideas if that suits your
strict moral working code better."

He'd meant it as a joke, but he knew the minute the
words left his mouth that the moment they'd shared—
their first truly genuine one—was over.

"Sorry," she said shortly. "Maybe some other time."

Zach could have kicked himself, but there was no use
in wasting time on wishes. He simply nodded and tried
to unhook his seat belt, but it was wedged at an odd angle
beneath his thigh. "Can't seem to cut myself loose. If I
shift, could you unhook me?"

Dara's eyes narrowed as if to say, "Where's the trap
this time?" so he gave her his most sincere smile. "No
funny stuff, I promise."

"If you'd said scout's honor I'd have punched you,"
she responded. "Lift up."

He shifted as her small fingers brushed lightly against
the back of his thigh. He almost groaned in relief when
the seat belt sprang free. "Thanks," he said.

"No problem. I'd apologize for the cramped quarters, but—" She shrugged in mock sympathy.

Before Zach even thought about what he was doing,
he lifted a hand to her cheek and leaned across the small
space separating them. "It's not the cramped quarters I
object to," he said, tracing his thumb against her cheekbone.

FOUR

Zach paused, giving her a tiny window to pull away, to say no, to do anything that would bring him back to his senses and make him stop. He'd calmly, rationally decided to pursue this during the long sleepless night after that first meeting in her office. But somehow, he'd envisioned being in control while doing it.

He wasn't. Not even close.

And she simply stared at him.

Then her lips parted, and he couldn't wait another instant. He slid his hand to the nape of her neck and pulled her mouth to his. His first taste lingered at the tentative brush of her palm against his chest. He wanted to sink his tongue deeply into the sweet, hot recesses of her mouth; to feel, taste, and touch all of her, all at once. But restraint made it twice as good, so he dipped a little, coaxing her back into his mouth.

The first touch of her tongue on his made his uncomfortable position in her cramped front seat almost unbearable. But instead of stopping he wove his other hand into her hair, angling her mouth so he could deepen the kiss.

His heart was pounding, his blood roaring in his ears, making him feel like he was in a free fall from outer space with no parachute or safety net to catch him before he crash-landed.

And he didn't give a damn.

It was only the realization that this was moving too fast—and that the backseat wouldn't hold them both—that forced him to stop.

Foreheads touching, both took a moment to allow their rapid breathing to slow. Dara was the first to shift away, and Zach let her go.

After another long moment Dara turned back to him, a small, tentative smile on her lips.

He fought the urge to reach for her again. Damn if he'd *ever* felt this way before, all shaky and uncertain, and so edgy, he could climb right out of his skin. He'd scaled jagged rocks with only his bare hands for support, skied steep mountains on a surfboard, dived off cliffs into rock-strewn waters, leapt from planes with only a triangular piece of nylon above his head.

None of it compared to this.

"I thought you said no funny stuff," she said, the rough quality of her voice belying her attempt at humor.

Zach ran a finger over her kiss-swollen lips. They were warm and damp. Damp from him. And just knowing that something of him still clung to her, made him even harder. God he wanted her so bad, he hurt. He was even more disconcerted when she didn't move away from his touch.

"What we just did was a lot of things, Dart. But it wasn't funny."

The intensity in his voice, in his eyes, made Dara look away again. She watched the steam on the windows evaporate, wishing her mind would clear as quickly.

"Dara?"

His voice was gentler now, yet that only emphasized the vulnerability and fear she thought she'd heard just seconds ago. No, she must have been mistaken. Zach Brogan, scared of a little kiss? Not in this lifetime.

It was wishful thinking on her part because she was feeling all those things and didn't want to be alone. Worst of all was the idea that it had been just a little kiss to him. She'd kissed and been kissed by other men since Daniel. Some of them had been passionate. But this. . . .

He made her feel wild and reckless, when she was no longer either of those things. No longer drawn to those traits in others. It evoked images in her mind of him jerking her clothes off, his mouth and hands on the rest of her body, of how it would feel when his bare skin touched hers for the first time.

No. It was no little kiss.

Praying her thoughts were not being broadcast through her eyes, she took a shallow breath and lifted her gaze to his. "What?"

"Is dinner still out of the question?"

She felt a small tug near her heart and smiled. "I really should get back to work." Was it her imagination, or was there a flash of relief in his eyes? That stung more than she cared to admit.

She shifted in her seat, taking the steering wheel with

one hand and putting the other on the gear shift. "Just give me a call, or have Beaudine call, and set up an appointment when you get the rest of the trip planned."

Another endless second elapsed, but she refused to look at him again. Out of the corner of her eye, she saw his hand lift, then drop back in his lap. Good, she didn't want him to touch her now. Did she?

"I have a trip to bid on and another one scheduled to leave this week. I'm not heading it, so I should have the rest of this together no later than the middle of next week."

She merely nodded in response.

After another pause, he said, "Dara?"

Please don't make me look at you again, she thought desperately. *Just leave and let me regroup here.* Even as she thought it, she turned to face him. "Yes?"

"Thanks for the ride," he said sincerely.

Everything would be okay, she assured herself. This had just been one of those weird moments they'd both quickly forget. She didn't really want Zach.

He'll go back to teasing me and flirting with me as he does with all the women he comes into contact with. And I'll go back to—I'll just—

Zach got out of the car and shut the door then leaned down, and rapped his knuckles once on the closed window. She looked over automatically in time to see him wink before he sauntered across the parking lot.

The rest of her breath departed on a loud sigh. *Yes, he'll go on teasing me and flirting with me,* she thought again as she watched him disappear behind another row of cars.

"And I'll keep being more turned on than I've ever

been in my entire life," she finished out loud. She could really hate him for that. "I'm an idiot," she muttered. Kiss or no kiss, she really didn't want to go back to work, and kiss or no kiss, she really wanted to spend more time with Zach Brogan. A whole lot more time. Maybe masochist was a better description.

She jerked the car into reverse and peeled out of the lot. The longer she was around him, the harder she knew it would become to remember all the reasons she had for not getting involved with a wild man again. That type simply didn't appeal to her anymore. Not really.

Slow and steady. Stable. Those were the kind of men she chose to date now. A man who'd grown up and learned to take responsibility for his life and for the lives of those he loved. A man more committed to home, hearth, and a nice nine-to-five job, than to looking for the next high, the next joyride. That only led to foolish risk. To tragedy. To pain. Especially for the ones left behind.

And Zach was far from slow and steady. His motto was live for the moment. He'd seen her as an unattached, consenting adult. Someone to play with for a while.

But a man like Zach wasn't cut out for the long term or stability, much less taking any sort of responsibility for those he cared about or those who cared for him.

And if she let herself get involved with him, in any way, no matter what rationale she used to protect herself, Dara knew that when the fall came, she would be the one not wearing a parachute.

Saturday was the sort of bright sunny day that made staying inside feel like a criminal offense. Dara shifted her attention away from her window and back to her desk. Her paper-strewn, folder-filled desk. She sighed, and pushed her chair back. She loved her job. It fulfilled her professional needs and her personal ones. But today her stable, steady life felt a whole lot more like dull and boring. Maybe a cola would help her focus on the reports she had to fill out.

"That and not wondering every other second what Zach is doing with a perfect summer day like this," she muttered. She stopped several feet from the door. "Oh, the hell with this."

She spun back to her desk, stacked the most urgent third of the pile into a canvas tote, then grabbed her purse and marched out of her office before common sense reemerged.

Guilt began to creep in as she neared the front door, making her glance around, despite the fact that she knew she was the only one there that day. The feeling vanished the second she pushed through the door. The warm breeze brushed her skin, and the blinding sun made her shade her eyes as she locked the heavy plate glass doors.

"I'll work tonight," she promised herself, her mind already sailing away on thoughts of what she would do first. The day seemed full of endless possibilities.

Music suddenly blasted through the air, making her jump. She barely held on to her tote bag. The tune was instantly recognizable, and she couldn't stop the grin that stole over her face as Roy Orbison belted out, "Oh, Pretty Woman."

She scanned the lot, instinctively looking for the

black pickup, but except for her car, the area in front of the building was empty. Dara swallowed the pang of disappointment, then laughed ruefully at her fickle nature. Hadn't she spent a good part of every hour since she'd left him convincing herself to get him out of her life as soon as possible?

The music was most likely coming from the gym located in the row of industrial buildings directly behind the foundation. She shrugged and strolled to her car, feeling alive and more than a bit wicked for ditching work. Her hips naturally began to sway in a sort of exaggerated walk to the beat of the still-blaring music. And so what, there was no one around to see.

She tossed the canvas bag onto the passenger seat, started the engine, then lowered the windows and climbed back out to let some of the heat dissipate. She was lip-synching along with Roy, drumming on the roof of her car and swinging her hips when her car phone rang. She jumped guiltily and cast an automatic glance across the empty lot.

Another self-deprecating laugh escaped her as she sat gingerly on the edge of the still-hot leather seat and reached for the phone. Before she could say hello, a deep male voice rumbled in her ear.

"Julia Roberts, eat your heart out." Husky laughter followed her sudden intake of breath. "Playing hooky, Dart?"

"Zach?" She swung around, scanning the lot again, but still didn't see his truck. He had to be nearby. The music—

Dear Lord, he'd seen her strutting her stuff across the lot! Surprisingly, the idea that he'd watched her wasn't as embarrassing as it was . . . stimulating. She didn't welcome that bit of news.

"Third pillar to your right, Dara."

Zach moved out from behind the large round brick column and leaned back against it, cellular phone propped between his ear and his shoulder. He wore a black baseball cap backward, a sleeveless white gym shirt, and black gym shorts that displayed a pair of tanned, well-muscled thighs. For some reason, her gaze strayed to his crossed ankles with sloppy socks and loosely laced black leather high-tops.

She stifled an unexpected giggle. Either it was hotter in the car than she'd thought, or she'd definitely been cooped up for too long if she was being turned on by a pair of oversize beat-up sneakers.

The heat in her cheeks began a swift downward rush, and she lifted her gaze back to his face only to find that sin-sexy smile. There was something about staring at him from the confines of her car that felt strangely . . . safe. Her reaction to the wink he sent her way, however, didn't come within spitting distance of safe.

"It's Saturday," she answered his question finally, speaking into the phone. "I don't think you can legally play hooky during non-business hours."

Zach pushed away from the pillar and strolled toward her car, the phone still at his ear. "And here I thought you didn't have any non-business hours."

"I just came in to get a few things that I need to review over the—" She broke off. "Why am I defending myself to you? You wouldn't know a business hour if you tripped over one, so who are you to go—"

"Don't go fire breathing again, Dart, it's too hot for

that already." He'd leaned down and propped his elbows on her open passenger door window, still talking into the phone—which somehow seemed endearing rather than silly.

Then he opened the passenger door, tossed her tote to the backseat, and got in. He threw his baseball hat on the dash, then hung up her phone. "And don't tell me you haven't been here all day. I've been calling your house since seven o'clock this morning."

"You've been calling? At my home?"

"Of course at your home. Which is where, silly me, I thought you'd be on a Saturday."

"You called at seven on a Saturday? You could have woken me up!"

"I won't say the thought didn't cross my mind, say, a dozen times or so." He wiggled his eyebrows. "Accompanied by some pretty vivid mental images, too, I must say."

"No, you mustn't say," she shot back hastily. This was already getting out of hand. And did he have to fill up her car with his tanned muscles and windblown hair and . . . and white teeth?

"Why were you calling me?" she asked. "You wouldn't by any chance be backing out and letting me know about the decision as soon as possible, would you?"

His wounded expression was entirely too convincing, and for a split second she actually wished she hadn't sounded so excited by the prospect of his quitting. Of course, if he had even an inkling about how easily he did excite her. . . .

"Actually, no," he said. "And before you ask, I got your home number from Dane."

"Such an accommodating brother." Dara made a mental note to spray paint her twin's private number on the next overpass she came to. "What was so urgent you had to talk to me on a weekend?"

"You said to call when I had the trip finished. When I couldn't get you at home, I figured you were at work. I tried that, but—"

"The switchboard is shut down during the off-hours."

"Which I learned after listening to the recording. So I started dialing your car phone as I headed this way, figuring I'd either get you here or catch you in your car somewhere."

"I won't even ask how you got this number. When I see Dane—"

"Can't collar him with that one. I memorized it from our ride the other day."

"Oh." Why did she feel sort of flattered by that tidbit of information? Dangerous thoughts, Dara. "What if I hadn't been working?" she asked, wanting—needing—to knock him down a peg. "I might have been out with someone else. I mean, it is a nice day. I could have been on a picnic."

"You could have been. But you weren't. You were working."

"And now I'm not," she said evenly. "So tell me why you're here, so I can enjoy the rest of my day off."

His expression made it clear he didn't think she had the first clue about enjoying herself. "Actually, I was hoping I could convince you to put in a few more hours. Only I promise it'll be a whole lot more fun, and you won't have to be indoors."

"Bottom line, Zach. What do you want with me?" she asked.

The humid air suddenly seemed too thick for breathing. Zach's expression went from teasing to predatory in a heartbeat.

"Dangerous question, Dart. Sure you want to know?"

Dara nodded.

His gaze locked on hers. "I think that what I want from you would take hours, maybe even weeks, to discuss." Then he laughed quietly and shook his head. "For today, I'd just like to request the pleasure of your company—in a professional capacity—to look over the area I've designated for the trip."

Hours, weeks . . . Dara's imagination ran wild with images of what Zach would do with her for hours, weeks . . . Beads of perspiration trickled down her neck. It took a moment to remember his actual proposition.

"I . . . uh, you want to show me the area you've chosen? Is it a very long drive?"

"We're not going to drive."

Confused, she said, "Then you have a map or something?"

"It's sort of a surprise."

"A surprise?"

"Yeah, you know, that's when something happens that isn't expected or planned."

"I usually call them accidents or problems. I'm not much on either of them."

"Well, I can see you just haven't had the right sort of surprises." He grinned. "Dara, could I ask you just to trust me on this? It will only take a couple of hours. Please?"

His plea was too plaintive to ignore. He looked like a little kid, all his hopes right there in his big brown eyes. "And I get to stay outside?"

Zach breathed a sigh of relief, restraining the sudden urge to kiss her. She was going to go with him. He hadn't been sure he'd pull it off. "Yeah, this is the perfect way to enjoy a day like today."

Her wariness visibly increased. "Enjoy? And what do you mean by 'way'? I thought you said—"

"There isn't a law saying all business has to be conducted in an office, or for that matter, has to be boring and dull, is there?"

She flushed. He loved that.

"My work isn't dull and boring," she defended. "But—"

"No buts. You'll need to change clothes, though." He gestured to the simple skirt and blouse she wore. Only Dara would wear office clothes to work alone on the weekend. "Do you want me to follow you home?" Dilated pupils now accompanied her flushed cheeks. "Why Dart," he admonished. "If I didn't know better, I'd think you might prefer an indoor . . . meeting." Zach easily deflected the punch she delivered to his shoulder. "Okay, I'm easy. You want to be outside, I could find a nice secluded spot." He wasn't quite fast enough to avoid her elbow before it jabbed into his ribs. His wince quickly changed to laughter.

After a last-ditch effort at frowning at him, she gave up and laughed too. "You are completely incorrigible, you know that?"

"Yeah, so I've been told. But I can usually control it better." He leaned closer. "Something about being around you, I guess."

Dara snorted. "Well, you certainly never worked too hard to control yourself when we were kids."

Zach laughed. "True, true. But back then I was a jerky kid who had no idea what to do with a girl who intrigued me."

"I intrigued you?" She smiled dryly. "You had a funny way of showing it."

"Yeah, well, at the time, I don't think I realized what made me do all those things to you."

"And now you do?"

"From the moment I opened your office door and saw you standing there, I knew exactly what made me do all those stupid things as a boy."

Dara feigned shock. "You mean it wasn't because your parents dropped you on your head as a child?"

Zach chuckled. "No. At least not that I know of." After a few seconds during which his body raced well ahead of his thoughts, his smile slowly faded. A moment later, hers did too. "Can I ask you something?"

She nodded.

"If you had been on a picnic today, is there someone special you would have gone with?"

He'd taken her by surprise again. Good.

"You tried to get me to answer this once before."

He shrugged. "Incorrigible. Your word."

"No, no one special," she said quietly. Her smile was shy, and completely captivating.

He reached over and pushed the tousled hair from her forehead. "I'm not a boy anymore, Dart," he said. "I still do some stupid things every once in a while, but I'm fairly certain I can make it through the rest of the afternoon acting like an adult. I can even throw in the picnic. Will you come with me?"

She didn't answer right away, and those few uncertain seconds sent another shot of adrenaline through his system. Just being around her, laughing with her, talking with her. Taunting her, teasing her . . . and Lord knew, kissing her. He never knew what to expect, like an ongoing thrill, a challenge of the sort he'd never confronted before.

"Okay. And if you want to know the truth, within seconds after I saw you again, there was no doubt in my mind you were an adult."

Zach felt his mouth drop open. He slid his hand to the back of her neck and tugged her closer to him. "Yeah. Now, instead of a hormone-confused boy stumbling around after you, you've got a completely intrigued adult male on your hands. Any ideas what you want to do with him?"

He brushed his mouth against hers, waiting for her, knowing she had to be part of the decision. Wanting her fully willing or not at all. And needing her to choose him more than he could have thought possible.

She looked in his eyes, then lifted her hand to his neck. Her gaze dropped to his mouth the split instant before she closed the remaining distance.

There were no preliminaries. The kiss began hot and wild and progressed swiftly from there. Her mouth and tongue weren't shy about finding his. She took what she wanted, and Zach willingly gave it to her. His hands dropped to her shoulders. His tongue moved deep into her mouth as he slid his palms down across her breasts, groaning as he felt her respond against his fingertips.

His hands drifted to her waist, and he'd half pulled her across the console separating them and into his lap when she began to pull back.

"Zach," she murmured against his mouth. "Zach."

He pulled his mouth from hers, then traced kisses across her jaw until his face was tucked into the sweet-smelling crook of her neck. "Yeah?" he said roughly.

She leaned back until she could look at him, and brushed a tangle of his hair from her face. Zach felt his body twitch in response to the one strand that clung to her lips. Again, the evidence of him on her rode hard against the need for restraint. He reached up and tugged it loose.

"What are we doing here, Zach?"

"Is there somewhere you'd rather go?" His smile was lost in the hoarseness of his voice.

"You know what I mean," she answered softly. "What's happening? I'm not . . . I mean, I don't usually . . ."

"You don't usually jump men in your car?" The banter came naturally to him, but he had to work at the casual tone. He didn't want to say anything serious because he might screw it up, yet he couldn't just joke around with her. What he was feeling was no joking matter. Not this time. For the first time.

"No, I don't," she answered with a hint of sexy confidence he hadn't seen before. "Well, not on Saturdays anyway." With studied nonchalance, she blew on her fingernails then held them out in front of her for inspection. "I usually reserve car sex for alternate Tuesdays."

Zach almost choked, then burst out laughing. "Damn, and here I was thinking I was going to be able to live out my autoerotic fantasies with you." He pulled her close and whispered, "You busy this Tuesday? I'll rent a limo."

Now it was her turn to laugh, making it impossible for him to resist taking another kiss.

"I don't know what we're doing," he whispered, pulling her head down to his again. He kissed her softly, gently, her responding moan followed closely by one of his. He pulled back while he still could and rested his head on the back of the seat. "Actually, I'm really enjoying what we're doing," he admitted. "Best business meeting I've ever had."

He pulled her to him and kissed her again, wanting to drag out the moment, to keep her off balance, keep her wanting more. He tasted her lips, her chin, her throat. Her arms circled his neck, and she returned his attentions. They were quickly lost again, the teasing kisses swiftly consumed by hungry ones.

Many seconds later, Dara pulled away. Their gazes caught and held, the silence only disturbed by their deep breathing. He lifted his hand and traced her cheekbone. She let her fingers weave into the hair against his neck. The silence spun out as they continued to stare at each other.

It hit him how infrequently, if ever, he made true eye contact with a woman. And when the bond went both ways . . . It was an amazingly intimate act. He'd never felt quite so open and vulnerable. Going stark naked in public would have been easier.

A tentative smile crossed her lips, but faltered a bit

when she spoke. "Zach, about this . . . whatever it is we're doing." Her smile strengthened when he raised his eyebrows. "I'm serious. I think we should discuss it. I'm not sure if this is wise. Especially if I'm going to be working with you"—she raised her hand at his questioning look—"however briefly. We have to set some boundaries."

"I don't do real well with boundaries, Dart."

FIVE

Dara started to talk again, but Zach cupped her chin and pressed his thumb gently against her lip. It quivered at his touch. "And I think we could set all the boundaries we wanted to and it would be a wasted effort." He rubbed his thumb back and forth. She gasped. "Be honest, Dara. Don't you?"

She sighed, blowing warm, sweet air against the pad of his thumb that he felt all the way to his toes.

She leaned away. "I guess I just can't figure out what it is you want from me. Besides the obvious," she added at his incredulous look.

He wondered if she'd asked herself the same question. He was trying hard not to. "Do we have to make a list? Analyze the whys and hows? I know you're a responsible, sensible person and, while you probably have a hard time believing it, so am I."

Her lifted eyebrow spoke volumes about her feelings on that subject. Zach had to laugh. He'd dated his share of women, some from different countries, different cultures. The one similarity was that most of them were as seduced by what he did for a living as by him personally. He'd never spent too much time trying to separate that perception. After all, the end result was the same, right?

But now . . . well, he knew Dara was turned on by him. Lord knew, the feeling was intensely mutual. But he couldn't recall a time he'd felt this need to defend what he did, or who he was. Dara wasn't hiding from the truth that something was happening between them. But she'd made it clear from the start that it wasn't his occupation that intrigued her.

Well, he wasn't going to sit there and defend himself. Besides, she'd always been more of a show-me person. He doubted that had changed. Which was fine by him. He'd always been more of a do-it person, himself.

"Come with me today." It was neither question or command. "No more pressure. I'll let you set the pace."

She shifted from his lap and settled back in her seat. He let her go with more regret than he'd expected to feel.

"I said I would," she responded finally, after adjusting the air-conditioning vents and putting on her seat belt. She looked over at him. "Lead the way."

The tousled hair and kiss-softened lips that accompanied her all-business tone and posture were damn erotic. "I'm parked around the corner. I'll follow you home and wait while you change." His body was still rock-hard. The image of her undressing did little to help that. "You do own a pair of jeans and a T-shirt, right?"

The dry smile crept back. "Sure. Hip-huggers and flower-power T-shirts are still in style, right?"

Zach laughed. "Shop that often do you? I don't care

what you wear." *I'll want to take them off you just the same.*
"Dress for comfort."

She nodded, and he ducked out of the car before she
could change her mind. Before he hauled her back in his
lap and said to hell—or heaven, actually—with the rest of
the afternoon he'd planned.

Dara placed her sneakered foot on the running board
and hiked herself up into the cab of Zach's truck. George
Thorogood blared from the speakers.

"Born to be wild and bad to the bone." She shot him
a tentative look. "How appropriate."

Zach turned the volume down to a level that wouldn't
damage their hearing, pulled a U-turn in the middle of
her quiet neighborhood street and headed back out to
the main highway.

"Nice house," he commented once they were heading west on Route 50. "When did you buy it?"

Dara smiled at his automatic assumption that she
wasn't a renter. "About four years ago. I shared a condo
in Fairfax while I was in college." She paused, not sure
how much she wanted him to know. It was obvious Dane
had never spoken of that time in her life to Zach. "Eventually I bought out the other half," she went on carefully.
"I liked the place and hadn't really planned on moving.
But mortgage rates dropped and resale values finally
went up, so . . ."

"A sound investment."

Dara glanced over at him, unsure if he'd meant that
as a jab. "So, you never got a place of your own?" He

darted her a quick look. The shadowed memories fled as she smiled sweetly. She could still parry with the best.

He didn't seem the least embarrassed. "Well, you probably remember that my folks were a bit older than most. Dad's asthma and Mom's arthritis sort of hit an all-time low when I was in college. They decided to retire to New Mexico right after I graduated, so I took over the house."

"Dane never really said much." She didn't say that she'd spent a good part of that time of her life sitting beside a bed in the intensive care unit of the hospital, wondering how life could be so incredibly unfair, for once not too interested in what was happening in her brother's life. She forced the memories back into their dark corner. "How are they doing?"

"Better than ever," he said. "Mom finally edged Dad out of the top three at the golf club." He glanced over at her briefly. "They started letting her play with the men when she beat the club pro. The ex-club pro."

Dara laughed. "Now I know which half of the gene pool you came from."

His laughter joined hers. "Yep. And damn proud of it. How about you? Your mom and stepdad still living in North Carolina?"

"Yes. Retired life seems to suit them. Mom is heavily involved in community projects, and Stan seems content to putter around the house and garage." Yes, her mother was truly content. And who wouldn't be with a man like Stan? Dependable, always around when you needed him. The riskiest thing he did was to climb onto the roof once a year to put up Christmas lights.

"Another dream come true," Zach commented.

Dara stared out the window, past the fields to the blue-purple shadow of the mountains on the horizon. "Yeah," she said after a moment. "I guess you could say that." Her thoughts skipped past the endless heartbreaking cases she dealt with on a regular basis and returned again to that hospital ward. And all those dreams she'd watched die, day after day, including hers and Daniel's.

The bump of the tires over gravel brought her head up and thankfully gave her something else to think about. They had pulled off into the parking lot of an old boarded-up gas station. "Why are we stopping?"

"We're here." Before she could question him, he'd switched off the ignition and hopped out of the truck. Seconds later her door swung wide and Zach held out his arms to her. She reached for his hands. He reached for her hips, and he lifted her down.

He captured her mouth for a quick, hard kiss just as her feet touched the ground. He was gone, moving to the back of the truck before she could call him on it.

She knew she should put a stop to that sort of hit-and-run behavior right from the start. But she let it go for now as she followed him. What the hell, it was just a kiss.

Zach chose that moment to wink at her. *Bad to the bone.*

And what bones they were. She stifled a sigh. Just a simple kiss, huh?

He lifted a huge cooler from the back, his muscles rippling and bunching with the effort.

"Call me crazy," she said a moment later, resisting the urge to fan her skin, "but I don't think camping in a parking lot under the shade of the ol' diesel pump is exactly what the kids had in mind."

Zach started across the lot, the cooler bouncing against his thighs.

"Oh, ye of little faith," he said.

Dara followed him as he neared the side of the dilapidated building. She stumbled to a dead halt after rounding the corner. In an overgrown field was a large rainbow-colored hot-air balloon.

As if sensing she was no longer behind him, Zach turned back to her. "Beautiful, isn't it?" When she didn't answer, he closed the remaining distance between them. "You don't have a thing about heights, do you?"

She finally pulled her gaze away and looked at him. "Heights? Me?" She looked at the balloon again, then back at him. "Nah." Her attention returned to the balloon. "Ferris wheels, roller coasters, tall ladders, piece of cake." *Flying, on the other hand, scares me silly.*

"Great. Come on, I want to introduce you to a few of my crew. They'll be part of the trip."

That managed to get her attention. Visions of making herself actually climb into that tiny basket were put mercifully aside for a moment. "Which trip? Today, you mean?"

"No, today they're just doing the setup, the tracking and the takedown at the end. I mean, the camping trip. These are the guys I'll use." At her frown, he smiled. "If you approve of the trip, Ms. Colbourne, ma'am," he added.

She couldn't stifle the smile at his obeisant tone and slight bow. Zach was a man who bowed only to the direction of the wind and the ebb and flow of the tide.

And, she thought with a private thrill, for the next week or so anyway, to her.

"Shall we?" He nodded in the direction of the hot-air balloon.

Her smug feeling vanished. She needed to tell him she couldn't go up in that thing, and she needed to do it now, when she'd only humiliate herself in front of him and not half his crew as well. "I'm right behind you," she heard herself say instead.

She waded through the wake he created in the hip-high grass, trying to ignore the melancholy feeling that accompanied this most recent reminder of just how incompatible they were. It went beyond his day-at-a-time attitude and her need for long-term responsibility, beyond his endless search for the ultimate thrill and her need to establish stability.

Oh, what the hell, she thought in disgust. If she got any more involved with him, fear of losing life or limb would probably keep her from going on half the dates he'd plan anyway, so worrying about the big picture was probably premature.

A young blond man met them about ten yards from one of the thick ropes anchoring down the balloon. "Hi, I'm Scotty!" He took the cooler from Zach and flashed her a smile that would have put the entire Osmond clan to shame. "You must be Dara," he said, putting the cooler down long enough to give her a brisk handshake.

Scotty's exuberance was a tangible thing—probably the result of an overdeveloped adrenal gland—but contagious nonetheless.

Dara grinned and nodded. "Hi. Pleased to meet you."

"Stow that in the gondola, would you, Scott?" Zach asked, gesturing to the cooler.

"Sure thing, boss."

Scotty loped away, and Zach put his arm lightly around her shoulders, steering her toward the Jeep parked near the balloon. "Come on, I'll introduce you to the guys."

Dara's feet remained rooted to the spot. As far as she knew, vertigo usually occurred looking down from a high place. Which did little to explain why she had a sudden wave of dizziness when she took in the full scope of the hot-air balloon. Her gaze lowered slowly over the massive billowing cloud of rainbow stripes and landed with a mental thud on the tiny wicker basket that dangled below it.

"Uh, Zach, there's something we have to talk about."

"If it's about having the crew ready before I asked—"

He started forward as he spoke, and Dara had to duck out from under his arm to keep from being literally dragged along. He swung around to face her, his confused expression blessedly distracting her from the flying thimble.

"Dart?" He closed the distance between them until her line of vision was filled with his chest. "What's up?" He lifted her face to his with a finger under her chin. "Are you worried about spending time alone with me? Is that it?"

That he seemed so honestly concerned with how she felt about him didn't help her case. She tried for a cocky smile. "Well, an hour or two with you in an overgrown picnic basket could give new meaning to the words 'captive audience.' "

He leered suggestively at her, but the expression quickly faded to a warm, gentle smile that made her want to retally their incompatibilities.

"The appeal there is enormous, but I get the feeling this isn't about playing footsie at five thousand feet." He let his thumb drift over her bottom lip. "What's really wrong?"

Five thousand feet? She swallowed. Hard.

"I didn't lie about being able to handle amusement park rides and the occasional tall ladder." She pulled back from his touch and looked down for a second. "Anything attached to the ground is no problem. Flying on the other hand . . ." she added sheepishly.

She could feel the heat in her cheeks and hated it. She felt as if they were back on the playground and she'd just been forced to admit defeat to him. What was worse was the compulsion to turn and run for the truck. She took only minor satisfaction in conquering it.

"Is it because of your dad?" he asked gently.

She studied the individual blades of grass waving in the breeze around her hips. "I don't know. Maybe. Probably. I've never really analyzed it."

"You? Not analyze something?" he teased gently. "I refuse to believe it."

She didn't have to look up to know her halfhearted punch had landed squarely in his stomach. He didn't flinch, neither did his abdominal muscles. "I tried once. I hated it," she said, amazed that instead of crying, she was fighting the urge to laugh. How did he do that? "It's never been an issue since, okay?"

"Until now, huh?"

She met his gaze. "Just the thought of getting even a

foot closer to that thing makes me queasy. I'm sorry about this, Zach." She waved her hand. "You went to a lot of trouble."

"Don't be. It's my fault. It just didn't occur to me."

The melancholy wave threatened again. Not that he could have known. He still thought of her as the wild child he'd grown up with. But that didn't keep her from wondering what else "just didn't occur" to him in his zeal for making plans and chasing thrills. There was no denying Zach was a successful businessman. But his business was about taking risks, and consequences be damned. The kids she worked with already faced too many risks and had dealt with too many consequences. And frankly, so had she.

A dull throb took up a slow tempo behind her eyebrows.

"What do we do now?" she asked quietly.

Zach read concern, worry, and fear in her eyes. He wished like hell he knew what was going on inside her head. He could almost hear the wheels turning. Somehow he doubted she was thinking about the balloon ride or the camping trip. He had the distinct impression her thoughts dealt specifically with him—as he related not just to her job, but to her personally.

He could always just come out and ask. But he wasn't particularly interested in having that fact confirmed.

"What we're going to do, is go on a picnic. That's one promise I made that I can still keep."

"But you don't have to—"

"Yes, I do." Zach saw she was about to argue and ended it the fastest way he knew how. With his mouth on hers. She stiffened at first, but only seconds later her lips softened, and Zach had to stifle a groan and the urge to pull her into his arms. While he still could, he broke off the kiss and leaned his mouth close to her ear. "I want to, Dara." He dropped a kiss on the soft skin just below her earlobe. His heart was pounding. Her light scent filled his head, the rush finer than the thin air at twenty thousand feet.

"Besides," he added. "We need to go over the plans for the camping trip." He barely waited for her to nod before heading across the field to Scotty and the rest of the ground crew.

They were back in the truck and heading farther west, the soft outline of the Blue Ridge Mountains dominating the skyline ahead of them, when Dara finally broke the long silence.

"It was really beautiful, Zach." At his questioning look, she clarified, "The balloon, I mean. Is it yours? Your company's?"

"No, it belongs to a friend of mine. I rent it from him occasionally for trips with clients." He shot another look at her. "Today was a loan from one friend to another, Dara, so don't worry. I knew I was taking a chance."

"I still feel bad about it. I'm sure my fear of flying seems pretty silly to someone like you." She glanced over at him, but his eyes were trained on the road. "We've set up a few balloon ride trips for kids at the foundation. I imagine it must be spectacular up there."

"It is." He reached across the seat and laced his fingers through hers. "Don't knock yourself for not liking to fly, Dart." He squeezed her hand before letting go to downshift at a red light. "It's not a fatal disease."

It wasn't fatal. Unless of course she found herself falling for a thrill-seeker. And then the only fatality would be her heart.

"How did you get into doing what you do?" she asked, hoping the answer would give her the strength she needed to resist him. Lord knew nothing else had.

"It was after you moved away. You know I loved sports, anything that demanded a physical challenge. In high school, none of the organized sports really did it for me."

"Not a team player? Now, why doesn't that surprise me?" She'd meant it as a joke, but a quick look at his face told her he'd taken her seriously.

"It wasn't that, Dara. I wondered about it though, being an only child and admittedly liking to be the center of attention. But there were solo sports too. None of them jazzed me. I tried it all. Football, basketball, tennis, golf."

"Golf?"

"Hey, I'll have you know I swung a mean five iron."

She laughed, certain he could have been captain of the team if he'd wanted to. "So what changed?"

"My parents took me snow skiing for the first time."

"Skiing?"

"Yeah, I was sixteen, and we went up to Vermont for Christmas break. I hit that first chairlift and zoom, I felt like I'd been launched into outer space. Scared me to death, but it pumped me too. Then coming down the hill. I don't know. I took to skis like I'd been born in them. Something about the speed and the wind and feeling like you were riding on the edge. One day, one mountain, and I was hooked."

"An adrenaline junkie is born. And here I thought you would've been more at home as quarterback or star pitcher, something where thousands would chant your name and stand and cheer." Like Daniel, she thought silently. Only he'd been hooked on the rush, too, just like Zach. Daniel tried it all. Nothing was too crazy. He was invincible.

Or so he'd thought.

Zach looked unrepentant. "Yeah, me too. But I wasn't. Testing myself, relying on myself that way—mentally, physically—did it for me."

"So why aren't you living in Colorado or the Alps?" she asked, purposely comparing him to Daniel, trying to find her way back to that nice, safe place she'd carved out for herself.

"Well, I didn't get to ski often, and around here it was a limited sport, anyway. So I began to hunt down other things that held the same excitement. I took skydiving lessons as soon as I was eighteen. Then hang gliding from a friend in college."

"I bet the bungee jumpers just loved you."

He laughed. "I switched my major to business management," he went on. "I started organizing trips for my frat house, and eventually one of the alumni took an interest and invested in me. The Great Escape just sort of blossomed from there."

"Well, you're obviously not alone in your addiction."

He slowed for the next light and looked at her as he came to a stop. "True. And I managed to turn it into a job I love and that I'm good at. I never planned it, but I don't regret a single minute of it."

She remained silent, his continued stare finally making her shift her gaze to the side window. "And you're still alive to say so." Dara bit her tongue at the sharpness of her words. The last thing she wanted to think about—talk about—was her past.

"You don't think much of me—personally, I mean—do you?"

"That's not true."

"Sure it is. You can't stand it that I'm not dedicating my life to a more worthy cause. To something of importance."

"You make it sound like you resent what I do. Isn't that reverse snobbism?"

"That's just it. I don't. It's obvious you love what you do. But so do I. And isn't that what's most important?" When she didn't answer, he added, "Do what makes you happy, hope it pays the bills. That's my motto."

She folded her arms. "And to hell with how it affects anyone else, right?"

Her heated response left him speechless. After a moment he shook his head. "Boy, lady, you're tough."

Dara looked away. "I don't always think so. But I'd like to be."

"What's wrong with enjoying your job, whatever it is? Would it be easier for you to accept me if there was some deep psychological reason for why I do what I do? Like some tragedy in my past I'm trying to escape from?"

Dara's wince was automatic and uncontrollable. The next thing she knew, Zach had zoomed through the intersection and pulled off the road onto the wide grassy shoulder.

He shoved the emergency brake on and propped one knee on the seat and draped his arm along the back. "Hey listen. Dara, whatever I said, I'm sorry."

"It doesn't matter, Zach." She looked at him. "Not really. I mean, it's a moot point. Beyond determining whether or not you are capable of setting up a trip to meet the foundation's specifications, how I feel about what you do really doesn't make a difference."

"It obviously does make a difference, Dara." He moved his hand to cup her head, playing gently with a strand of her hair. "Don't ask me why, I've never much cared what people thought of me. But your opinion matters a great deal to me."

Don't ask me why. No, she wouldn't. If she did, then he might ask the same question of her, or worse, she might ask it of herself. Because regardless of the fact that it shouldn't, Zach's opinion mattered to her too.

"Zach," she said finally, "you're a good friend to Dane. You and Jarrett. My brother didn't always make friends easily."

"Yeah, he was the quiet, studious one. More like your mom."

"After we moved to Fairfax, Dane never really had friends like you and Jarrett again. I guess that's why he's worked hard to keep in touch with you guys over the years."

"His friendship is important to me too. And now that I've met you again, so is yours."

His fingers drifted to her neck. "That's my point."

She pulled away. "I think it would be better if we just concentrate on business and keep this as a friendship."

Zach's brown eyes probed hers for a long, silent moment. She didn't turn away. Finally, he said, "One of the things my occupation has taught me is that I'm very good at concentrating on more than one thing at a time. And I have no intention of losing your friendship."

"Zach—"

He moved across the seat, capturing her head between his hands. His mouth was gentle and requesting on hers. Asking her to respond, to be honest with him . . . with herself.

Just as she leaned into his kiss, Zach pulled back. He'd hit the edge the moment their lips had touched and knew if he didn't back away now, he'd sail off and take her with him.

His gaze strayed out the window, then back to her. He gestured to the truck interior. "Am I the only one who sees a definite pattern emerging here?" He'd tried for humor, but the words sounded rough. Damn, why did everything with her seem so important? He couldn't escape the feeling that he was walking on a narrow ledge and that if he wasn't careful, some unseen shove would send him tumbling off with nothing but air as his safety net.

He took one look at her glassy eyes and felt a distinct nudge.

"This is hopeless, Zach." She braced her hands on his shoulders. "It is. We weren't compatible as kids, and we're even more incompatible now. You leap before you look, and most of the time I don't even make it to the edge."

"You're wrong. The reason we didn't get along as kids was because we were too much alike. You're still one of the bravest people I know. What you face every day. When we were kids you never gave in. You always stood up to me even at my worst. You're standing up to me now." He covered her hands with his, pulling them from his shoulders. "I know you think I'm irresponsible, but I really do look first. There is no room for error in most of the things I do, so I calculate risks, measure the odds." His lips curved. "Dead clients don't make great repeat customers, and word of mouth doesn't work too well from beyond the grave."

Dara fought to breathe past the sudden knot in her throat. No. She wouldn't repeat past mistakes. She'd been young, inexperienced, and feeling a bit immortal herself when Daniel had swept into her life. But his effect on her could be described as a mild breeze compared with the hurricane force of one Zach Brogan. She felt about as futile as if she were fighting a real one single-handed.

"You know what I'm saying, Zach," she persisted. "You keep thinking of me the way I was back then. I'm not that person anymore. You're still impulsive, I'm not. You're—"

"Getting tired of this line of discussion." He sighed as she tried to tug her hands from his, but held tight. "Okay, I can see I'm beating my head against the prover-bial wall here. And I know I have an entire childhood of stupid behavior to live down and an occupation that is admittedly not the standard nine-to-five gig."

"It's more than that—"

He tugged her closer. "But I also think there's still

more D'Artagnan in you than you're willing to admit. Yes, you've changed. So have I, even if you don't see it. I don't know why you climbed into the castle and pulled up the drawbridge behind you, but that doesn't mean we shouldn't spend time together. Get past the surface impressions, the childhood memories. Who knows, maybe we'll find out there's something more going on here than hormones with a bad case of spring fever."

She blew out a long, soft breath and lowered her head.

Keeping her hands locked under one of his, he tilted her chin up. "Or is that what you're afraid of?"

SIX

Zach saw the fear and resignation in Dara's eyes. It made his heart stumble.

"I'm just trying to be realistic," she said. "Yes, we could spend more time together. But I think our hormones have already made it quite clear how they want us to spend it."

"And is that really so bad, Dara?"

She looked him straight in the eyes and said, "I don't think I could handle it." She placed her fingertips across his lips when he would have spoken. "It's not all hormones. I do like you, Zach." A ghost of a smile curved her lips. "Which is something I'd never thought I'd hear myself say. And I know you're a loyal friend to Dane and Jarrett. I could use a friend like that. I don't want to risk losing that for a short-term affair, no matter how intense and wild it may be."

"And what if we can't be just friends, Dart?" he whispered roughly. "Wouldn't you rather take the risk of finding out that maybe what we have is bigger, brighter than we'd ever expected, than have nothing at all?"

He dipped his head slightly and pulled the tip of her finger into his mouth. She gasped, and he pulled her finger deeper into his mouth, exerting slight pressure, then let it slide out, before doing it again. He lifted his hand to her wrist, holding her there, then suddenly pulled her into his lap.

He let her finger slip from his mouth and lowered his face to hers. "Don't you think the decision is already out of our hands?"

Her breath was coming out in fast, short pants, her pupils were dilated to the point of swallowing her irises. His fingers pressed against her wrist absorbed the rapid rate of her pulse.

"No," she said, an almost desperate edge to her voice. "I . . . I can name another director . . . to handle the trip, I mean. We can walk away from this. And in a while we won't feel this way anymore."

He jerked her closer. "You really believe that? How long will it take, Dara? A day? A week? Another fifteen years?"

"I think maybe it's time you took me home."

"And I think you've finally walked back to the edge, Dart. Maybe it's time for you to leap."

Dara thought her heart might burst through her chest it pounded so hard. How had she let this happen to her again? She wanted him so bad right now that nothing, not even recalling the darkest moments of her past could help her.

But her self-preservation instincts must have been more deeply ingrained than she knew. Because before she could coherently decide on an action, she was scrambling out of his lap and over to her side of the truck. She opened her window and turned her face to warm air, taking deep, gulping breaths.

She'd been to the edge and survived. Somehow that realization wasn't nearly as empowering as it should have been. She didn't look at Zach.

He shifted the truck into four-wheel drive and headed out across the empty field, using the huge "land for sale" sign posted by the roadside as an open invitation to make himself at home.

He didn't stop until the road noise was a distant hum and the grass wheel-hub high. A broken-down fenceline, an old abandoned barn, and a topless silo were their only company. That and the soft rolling shadows of the Blue Ridge Mountains.

Zach dug out a blanket, spread it across the bed liner in the back and popped open the cooler. He appeared at her door a minute later, and without a word swung her into his arms and lifted her into the back of the truck in one graceful motion.

"Help yourself," he directed as he braced one hand on the open tailgate and vaulted into the back.

Dara took him at his word, more to give herself something else to concentrate on than because she was really hungry.

She discovered she was hungry as she yanked several aluminum-foil-wrapped packages and a six-pack of soft drinks out of the cooler and arranged them on the blanket. Starving in fact.

Talk about other things. That's what they needed to do. Discuss the camping trip, get him to tell her about some of the wild things he'd done. She could tell him about some of the wishes she'd seen fulfilled at the foundation. The sort of stuff friends would talk about. Talk. Period.

"I hope you like cold cuts." Zach took a bag of chips and a bunch of grapes from the cooler then flipped over the lid as a makeshift table.

"It all looks fine." They arranged their plates in silence, which was surprisingly free of tension. Maybe it was the warmth of the sun seeping into her bones, the languid, lazy feeling of being out in the middle of nowhere on a beautiful day. With the cooler between them, they both settled back against the black plastic storage compartment that was built in behind the cab and rested the plates on their stomachs. The last of her muscles uncoiled and relaxed. Maybe she'd finally gotten through to him. It wouldn't be so hard after all to keep things platonic.

"Dara."

She'd been staring up at the cloudless sky, concentrating on the soothing feeling of the gentle breeze on her skin and the heat of the sun on her face. Calm and unguarded, she turned to Zach. "Hmm?"

"Open your mouth."

"Wha—?" The question was cut off by a plump grape, which Zach pressed gently between her lips.

"Good, huh?"

She chewed the juicy fruit and nodded warily when his fingers remained on her lips a bit longer than necessary. She had to stifle the urge to lick them and catch his taste too.

"Have another." He leaned over her, casting her body in the shade.

She took the small bunch from his hands, popped the remaining three in her mouth, then handed him the empty stems. His grin was wide and free, and made her wish she hadn't been so quick to stop him.

No. Friends talked and laughed together. But she was fairly certain that they didn't feed each other.

"Sit up for a second." He motioned her forward, then shifted to his knees, and unlocked the storage compartment.

From her position she could see a few volleyballs, some rope, and some unusual-looking equipment she wasn't familiar with. Before she could ask, he pulled out a rolled-up, multihued bundle and a large spool of string then quickly closed the lid. With his foot, he shoved the cooler to the side of the truck and began to unfurl the colorful roll.

He smiled over at her as he stuck his finger in his mouth then held it up to the wind. "Perfect." He unearthed another old blanket, rolled it up and laid it in the truck bed along the front of the storage box.

"Lie down."

"I beg your pardon?" she said.

He smiled. "Just stretch out and relax." He reached over and flipped the sunglasses she'd pushed up on her head down to her nose. "You can do that, can't you?"

Dara bit her tongue; it was either that or give in to the impulse to stick it out at him, but she did as he asked. She was rewarded by his look of surprise. He'd expected her to be difficult. Amazing how easily they slipped back into their childhood roles of challenge me-challenge you.

Zach leapt gracefully over the side of the truck. She sat up and rolled to her knees.

"What are you doing?"

He looked over his shoulder. "I promised you a picnic, to keep you outside, and a business meeting that would be fun and not boring. But you're making it really hard." When she scowled, he just winked. "Now would you lie back down, please?"

"Yes, sir." It had been so long since she'd really relaxed and enjoyed herself. Usually she was in charge of making sure everyone else was relaxing and having fun first.

Lost in her thoughts, she gasped when a cloud of bold, vibrant color billowed up over her head. She watched, entranced, as the Chinese dragon kite caught the breeze and sailed upward. A quick peek showed Zach was yards away, working the line. When the brilliant streak of nylon appeard much smaller than she knew it to be, he came back to the truck.

"Here, hold this." He pushed the string roll at her.

"Me? I've never flown a kite."

He shoved the large plastic spindle into her hands, placing her thumb over the string to keep it from spinning out. "Now you have."

He grabbed a pair of aviator sunglasses from the dashboard and slipped them on, then hopped back into the bed of the truck. After quickly stowing away the remains of their lunch, he stretched out next to her, leaving just enough space between them so their elbows brushed together.

"It's beautiful."

Zach rolled toward her and braced his head on his hand. "Yeah, I know."

She frowned. "I was talking about the kite."

He lifted his shades, his expression one of mock confusion. "Who said I wasn't?"

Trying hard not to blush—something she'd done far too often since meeting him again—she turned her attention back to the sky and the dragon.

Zach rolled onto his back again, tucked his hands behind his head and crossed his ankles. "So, you want to hear about the trip?"

She laughed.

"What?" He lifted his head and looked over at her. "This is the business part of the promise." He grinned. "Or have you changed your mind about that part? Myself, I'd much prefer a personal conversation."

"Stick to business, Brogan. Personal is too dangerous around you."

She never saw the kiss coming. It was hard and fast and sent her heart soaring straight up with the kite. He broke it off before she could even begin to respond.

She blushed again when he reached over and placed her thumb back on the string which was peeling off the spool at a rapid rate.

She shoved the string roll at him. When he lifted his hands away, she said, "You told me you could concentrate on two things at once."

"I thought I already was." He grinned, but took over manning the kite.

After making sure he was settled back in a prone position, with his eyes on the kite, she relaxed herself. "You really are impossible."

"Actually, I'm very easy."

Dara snorted. "Talk, Brogan. Tell me about the trip."

He dropped a light kiss on her cheek. "Look, ma," he whispered, "no hands."

When she didn't say a word, Zach started laughing, and Dara joined him.

"Okay, point made. Give me the damn kite. But no more funny stuff. Friends, remember? You promised me a picnic and business. The former was lovely, thank you. Now, sell me on this trip."

"Hey, I thought they were pretty friendly kisses, didn't you?" Zach pulled his legs away just in time to avoid her well-aimed kick. "Okay, okay. Well, I'd like to leave next Friday," he said casually, tucking his hands behind his head. "I hope that won't be a problem."

Two days later Dara propped the phone between her chin and shoulder, counting the fourth ring. "Please Dane, be home."

"Colbourne."

"I've got five days to become a camping expert. You're in charge."

"Well, hello to you too." Dane's tone was serious as usual, but she heard the teasing quality that he reserved just for her. "A camping expert, huh? Who are we trying to impress?"

Dara really hadn't been looking forward to this part of the conversation, but knew it was better to just get it out of the way. "Impress isn't really the right word. More like reduce the chance of humiliation."

"Okay, you've got me intrigued. But if you know the

guy well enough to camp out with him, why haven't I heard about him?"

"We're thirty, Dane. Do you let me check out all your ladies before you spend the night with them?"

"This from the sister who just last month was telling me that I needed to get a life or get laid?"

"And have you?" she asked too sweetly.

"You think I'd tell you if I had? Ten minutes with you and a few childhood stories later, the poor woman would be running for the hills."

"Just what I thought," she replied knowingly. "Really, Dane, you work harder than I do. You really could use—"

"You're stonewalling, Colbourne," he broke in. "Who's the guy? Is it someone I know?"

Dara sighed. "Do I have to?"

"You want my help or not?"

"Zach Brogan."

Dead silence greeted her announcement.

"Dane?" She'd expected wild laughter or more likely, considering her brother had grown entirely too sober lately, a few well-intended jibes. "You still there? Don't make me say it again, it was hard enough the first time."

"Brogan?" he said finally. "You and Zach? Well, I guess I've finally lived to see it all. Talk about your final ironies."

"You're planning on calling Jarrett," she said. "I can hear the wheels turning. Well, don't. First off, McCullough will find out soon enough since it was his brilliant idea that got us together in the first place."

"Jarrett played matchmaker? Now I know I've entered a parallel universe. He'd be the last person on earth to meddle. Maybe this whole marriage thing went to his head."

"Dane, stop. It's not what you think."

"You and Brogan alone together on a mountaintop for anything longer than five minutes and it's exactly what I think. Are you sure about this?" he asked, his strident tone mellowing a bit. "It's not really like you."

She let that last comment pass. "We're going on business, Dane. Zach is planning a trip for the foundation that requires my approval."

"So there will be others with you?"

She paused, then answered honestly, knowing there was no point in hedging, since he'd just drag it out of her anyway. That was the downside of having a twin who was also an investigator. "No. But," she hurried to add when he tried to break in, "we'll have separate tents and everything. We're simply colleagues. He knows how I feel and—"

"How *do* you feel? Honestly. I mean, you guys haven't spoken since you were kids, and there was certainly no great affection between you then. As a matter of fact, isn't one of his teeth capped because of you?"

Dara wasn't ready to explain—even if she could—what her relationship was with Zach. "As for the tooth, he started it, so he deserved what he got. As to your other question, I don't know. Honestly." She knew she shouldn't ask, but she couldn't help herself. "And what did you mean, about us not being able to be alone without . . . you know. We're both adults."

"I guess I just know how he is with women. He's the kind of guy who could walk into the men's room and still find himself instantly surrounded by women. I just don't want you to mistake his . . . attentions for something they're not."

"I can't believe I'm hearing this." Dara laughed. "Don't you think I understand the difference between idle flirtation and . . . you know, something more serious?" It was precisely because she wasn't sure at all if she could tell the difference when it came to Zach, that she turned the tables back on Dane. "And he's your best friend, for goodness' sake—"

"And you're my sister. Come on, Dara. I know you date, but I could have given you the same advice you gave me."

"And if I took it, Zach Brogan would probably fill part of that advice quite admirably." She smiled at the strangled sound he made. "I can handle it, okay?"

There was a deep sigh on the other end of the phone. "Dane?"

"Yeah, I'm here. I know you're an adult, and I know you can take care of yourself. But I also know how immersed you've become in your work. You give everything to those kids."

"Look who's talking. I love my work, you know that."

"I do, and don't get me wrong, that's a wonderful thing. But dating one of the foundation's stuffy lawyers or that insecure guy from accounting—"

"Phil's not insecure," she broke in, "he's just shy."

"And safe."

Dara paused, at a loss for a comeback. "Well, one thing Zach Brogan isn't, is safe. So you should be thrilled."

Dane sighed. "I'm sorry, that was uncalled for. But

ever since Daniel died, you haven't been the same. You're quieter, more serious. Which isn't bad, but that's more like me than like you."

"Can you blame me, Dane?"

"You know I admire the hell out of you, facing what you did and how you've turned it into such a positive thing. It's just that when it comes to your own happiness, you tend to go for guys who don't, I don't know, challenge you. The sort of guys you wouldn't be in danger of falling for."

Dara didn't know what to say. As close as she and Dane were, he'd never spoken to her so candidly. And never about this. She felt her throat constrict and her eyes burn. He went on before she could respond.

"I guess I just think someone out there should be working at least half as hard as you do for those kids, making *your* dreams come true. And while I still think Phil from accounting isn't the right guy, neither is Zach Brogan."

Dara's heart swelled a bit at his tender words in her defense. He wasn't one for overt displays of emotion, quite the opposite. More often it was gruff displays of overprotectiveness. "I called for camping tips," she teased gently, "not advice for the lovelorn. Which I'm not, by the way. I've lost two men I loved very much. You of all people have to know that the very last person I'd fall for is a man who takes the sort of risks Zach does. We've agreed the past is past, and I think he'd make a nice friend—" She broke off when Dane uttered a few choice words under his breath. "I mean it, Dane. I realize this sounds impossible, all things considered, but I think he's a nice guy. A helpless flirt and a maniac with a death wish, but underneath, a nice guy."

"Dara," Dane warned.

"I can handle it, big-brother-by-all-of-one-minute. Now, do I have your help or not?"

He sighed. "Okay, I'll help. I've got to conduct a few interviews out at TRACON this afternoon. How about we meet in Tysons Corner around eight, okay?"

"Deal. And Dane?"

"Yeah, yeah, I know. I love you too. Just don't go getting yourself hurt. I'd hate like hell to have to kill my best friend."

Only Dara would pack for a fun weekend trip like she expected to traverse a war zone. Zach's gaze scanned over the equipment-laden truck bed as he backed into an open spot between two oak trees at the base of the mountain.

She'd been waiting at the curb, all decked out in her new hiking shorts and boots, standing in the middle of a pile of camping gear that any scout leader would sell his merit badges for, and shot him that I-dare-you look. He'd been a goner before he'd put the emergency brake on.

Hell, if he were honest, he'd probably been a goner since the first time she'd socked him back when they were six. He'd just been too young and stupid to know true love when it stared him right in the eyes. Of course, he could only see out of one of them at the time.

"Why are we stopping here?" she asked now, almost three hours later.

He glanced over at her as he put the truck in neutral and set the brake. "Because this is where the trail begins." He pointed to the old service road that zigzagged its way up the hill in front of them, disappearing into the trees before the third switchback.

He watched her scan the trail.

"If you're worried about the truck, don't be. This is private property."

"Private property?" She looked back at him, then waved him silent. "Never mind." Sighing as she unhooked her seat belt, she said, "Another example of how different we are, I guess. The kind of people I know are the sort that might own a small sailboat and a time-share condo in Ocean City. Your friends own mountains and hot-air balloons."

He shifted and let his arm rest on the back of the seat, tucking his fingers into a loose fist to keep from touching her. "This is a problem? What our friends do or don't own?"

She turned her attention back to the trail. "Not really, at least, not in and of itself. But it does go a way toward defining why we'd be better off as friends." Before he could comment, she laughed. "Besides, thanks to you, I guess I could now say I have friends with access to hot-air balloons and mountains. Makes for good conversation at cocktail parties."

Zach released his own seat belt. He wondered what she'd say if he told her he wasn't much for the cocktail party circuit. But he didn't think it was wise to give her more ammunition at the moment. She probably thought he was a party animal anyway.

Only time spent together would make her understand, show her who he really was beneath all those labels she was busy hanging on him to keep her distance, to ignore what was happening between them.

And he couldn't remember looking forward to spending time alone with another person as much as he had this weekend with her. Even his annual jaunts with her brother and Jarrett didn't give him this sense of anticipation, of expectation. Nothing had ever felt like this.

But the idea of being just a friend to her simply wouldn't jibe in his head. The thought of being near her without touching her, of laughing with her but never kissing her. He simply couldn't imagine it.

"Well, I guess we'd better get our packs set up." Zach opened his door, suddenly desperate for some fresh air and a little more space between them. Her voice stopped him with his hand still on the door handle.

"What do you mean, get our packs? I thought we'd take the truck up. I mean, I know the kids are going to ride up in their buggies on the real trip."

"Because they can't walk. We can. Isn't that why you bought the hiking boots?"

"The hiking boots were for hiking, not mountain climbing. You know, as in leave the campsite for a jaunt in the woods?"

"That's not all there is to camping." He slid out of the truck and started digging in the heap of gear for their packs.

She got out and spoke to him from the opposite side of the truck bed. "Correct me if I'm wrong, but isn't camping the part where you pitch tents and make a campfire? Who said anything about having to tote the campsite up a mountain on your back?"

Zach looked up. She was serious. He tried not to laugh. "First off, this barely qualifies as a mountain. Everest it's not. And secondly, just how did you think this stuff was going to get up there when we do this trip for real? Did you think the kids would take it on the buggies? There will barely be enough room to strap on their own stuff."

He watched her flush in embarrassment and anger. It made him want to vault the back of the truck in a single bound and take her in his arms until all that heat was channeled into an entirely different sort of passion. Until he made her understand how intrinsic that passion was to her entire self, until he convinced her that burying it didn't make it go away.

"I guess I thought your guys would take everything up ahead of time and we would hike up for fun. You know, for the kids' sake." Her voice dropped to a low grumble as she added, "Dane told me I was wrong about that part, but would I listen? Noooo."

Zach had been pulling his bedroll out from under her tent which—even rolled up—looked as if it would sleep at least eight. Her mumbled words stopped him cold. He looked up at her. "You went to Dane for help on this trip?"

She glared at him, then shrugged. "I've never done this sort of thing before," she said, obviously uncomfortable now, but determined not to back down. He felt a tug near his heart.

"And you asked Dane for some tips so you . . . what? So you wouldn't be embarrassed?"

"Which you can see worked very well." She sighed.

"Go ahead, laugh. I should have known better than to try and impre—"

Zach's smile spread to a wide grin when she broke off and began digging furiously in the back of the truck for who only knew what.

Walking around to her side, he stopped just behind her. He began to reach for her, but she must have sensed it, because she stiffened. He knew he shouldn't touch her, but he couldn't stop himself. "Come here."

SEVEN

Zach gently placed his hands on her waist and tugged her around to face him. He waited a minute, knowing her well enough to realize she was incapable of not meeting a challenge. Finally, she lifted her gaze to his.

"I'm flattered you went to so much trouble, Dart."

"I didn't go—"

"Shhh." He placed a finger on her lips, then left it there when the warmth of her skin gave him a slight rush. "Did you really think I would hassle you?"

She arched a brow. "What, you're kidding, right?"

His grin faded. Her ongoing low opinion of him hurt more than he cared to admit. "You could have just told me. I'd have been glad to help you. I just figured you'd camped before or I would have said something."

She pulled away from the finger he'd begun rubbing across her lower lip. "I'm here to look out for the kids' interests—they've never camped either. My expertise comes in knowing their needs. Yours is to make sure the trip meets them."

"Didn't your folks ever take you and Dane camping?"

"No. My dad was gone too much for anything like that." She looked away for a moment, then back at him. "And Stan is not exactly the outdoorsy type."

Zach frowned. Her tone had been dry and self-deprecating, but there was old pain under the surface of her words. "So I guess you missed out on a few other things as well, huh? Pretty tough for a kid like you. I bet you wanted to ski, sail, surf. Do it all." He slipped his hand into her hair and tilted her head back when she tried to look away again. "I'm sorry your dad didn't have time for you when he was alive, Dara. I'm sure he'd love to have done all those things with you. He loved challenge as much as you. Who knows, you'd probably be flying planes now."

She tried to jerk away from him, but he kept her gently yet firmly in his grasp.

"I loved my dad more than anything, you know that," she ground out. "But it was long ago. I don't resent anything about the time we spent together. And Stan is wonderful. He's made my mom incredibly happy."

Zach brought her face up to his again. "Is that what you're looking for then, a younger version of Stan? Someone safe?"

Her skin paled a bit, but it was anger not pain that lit her eyes now. "There's not a damn thing wrong with wanting security and stability."

"No," he answered calmly, "there isn't. But you're not your mom, Dara. And I think if you really wanted someone like Stan, you'd have married him by now."

"And I'm supposed to take marital advice from you?

The reigning king of commitment and responsibility?" she asked sarcastically.

Zach picked up her hand and pressed a soft kiss on her palm. She gasped. That was one way to break an impasse with her. "How did we get on the subject of your family?"

"Because I didn't want to deal with how idiotic I feel about packing enough camping supplies to outfit the Boy Scouts' annual jamboree?"

Her laugh had him drawing her closer, intending to pull her into a deep kiss. But she ducked away. He let her go, knowing now was not the time to push despite how badly he wanted to. There would be other times, other kisses. There had to be.

She rooted around and pulled out her sleeping bag. "Why didn't you say something to me back at my house?" she asked. "We could have left most of this stuff in my garage."

He leaned back on the truck beside her and crossed his arms. "Because you looked so cute and adorable in your new hiking ensemble, I didn't have the heart."

She made a face. "Cute and adorable. Now there's two adjectives every woman yearns to hear."

Zach leaned closer. "I have a whole list of words to describe you. You want to hear some more of them?"

She shot him a droll smile. "Since I'm fairly sure I'd be lucky if two out of the first ten would be complimentary, I think I'll cut my losses now."

He dropped a quick kiss on her nose. "You'd be surprised, Dara."

❖━━━━━━━❖

"That's mountain laurel." Zach pointed to the bushes lining the edge of the forest. "Those trees are yellow birch, and over there is some red dogwood. The firs around here range from eastern hemlock and balsam fir to white pine and red spruce. There's some late-blooming trillium." He pointed to the ground near a fallen log. "The blossoms start out pink and change to white."

Dara's boots were killing her, and she relished anything that would take her mind off her blisters, even listening to Zach detail every aspect of the flora which surrounded them. She didn't have the heart to tell him that it was all just foliage to her. Pretty, soothing foliage, but nothing she was interested in knowing about on a scientific level.

"How did you learn all this stuff?" She stopped and pretended to pick a stone out of the tread of her boot.

"My parents and I hiked parts of the Appalachian Trail and around Skyline Drive occasionally, and I remember some from my dad. The rest is just part of the standard research in putting together a trip."

Dara knew she'd stalled as long as she could, so she carefully stepped forward again, taking small pride in not visibly wincing in front of him. "You research the plants and everything?"

"Depends on the trip. Most of the time it pays to know what is indigenous to an area, not just to prepare for any inherent dangers, but also as a safety precaution."

"And partly because you love soaking it all up, right?"

He grinned. "Best education around."

His eyes took on a vibrancy, and his voice became

more animated as he spoke. The excitement and pleasure he took in his job was obvious. Even feeling like she did, his attitude was infectious. And for that very reason disquieting.

"You said something about safety precautions," she said. "You mean like if you got lost or stranded you'd know what was edible and what wasn't? That sort of thing?"

"Partly. In the mountains, even relatively small ones like these, storms can come out of nowhere and depending on where you are there can be flash floods and even snow or ice storms in the spring. And no matter where you are, you want to make sure you don't invade the turf of an animal who prefers his own kind to humans."

Dara laughed, albeit a bit nervously. "I guess when you travel to exotic locales that would come in handy."

Zach looked over at her. "Yes, but it also holds true in the States. Even here in Virginia."

"What animal could we possibly spook up here that would represent a danger? I mean, there is an occasional bear sighting, but even I know that doesn't happen often. So that leaves, what? Squirrels, deer, raccoons, bunny rabbits?"

"Snakes. The timber rattler, for one."

Dara stopped dead. "Snakes?"

"Yes, snakes." He stepped closer to her, his expression serious. "Don't worry," he deadpanned. "We're miles from a biology lab. No one will make you dissect one." He broke into a wide grin. "Or kiss one."

Dara thumped his chest. "Very funny, Mr. Macho Mountain Man. I'll have you know it wasn't myself I was concerned about. I was worried about the children.

Their mobility is limited, and they might not be able to move out of the way of danger in time."

Zach looked as if he was buying her story, until he started laughing.

"It's a plausible concern," she insisted.

"Come on, Dara, fess up. You don't like snakes."

She waited a beat, then let her shoulders slump in defeat. "Terrified is a better word."

"Well, I'm not too fond of them myself. And I doubt we'll even see one. But as long as we take the proper precautions, it won't be a real concern anyway."

Dara started to move up the trail again, but Zach's hand on her arm stopped her.

"You want to take a break? You know, just sit and absorb the scenery for a while?"

Dara smiled over at him, even though she realized now she hadn't been nearly as good at concealing her discomfort as she'd thought. "I hate to tell you this, but it all looks pretty much the same to me."

Zach took hold of her shoulders and turned her around, then slid her pack off. "Come on, there's a big rock over there with your name on it."

"Oh goody," she said dryly, glad to have the load removed, even if only temporarily. "And here I thought they were all in my shoes."

Zach's pack hit the dirt trail with a thud. Before she knew what was happening, he'd scooped her up in his arms and was striding off the path into the woods.

Dara didn't have time to struggle, she barely had time to duck her head toward his chest to keep the low-hanging limbs from beating her senseless.

His breath fanned her cheek as he ducked down to

avoid them too. "Sorry about that. But my hands are sort of full at the moment."

Dara smiled against his T-shirt. Damn him for being so . . . him. And then she became aware of his hands wrapped around her thigh just above the knee, and the other one just under her breasts.

Her breath caught at the image of how his hands would feel if they slid up her body. One of his large palms could completely cover her breast. She suppressed a shiver at the thought of how the rough, warm skin would feel against them.

He slowed, then stopped a few seconds later. She lifted her head and found him staring down at her. Instead of the cocky grin she'd expected to find, he wore an expression she could only describe as . . . hot.

She gulped, suddenly needing to moisten her throat. His eyes told her his thoughts mirrored hers.

A small noise escaped her mouth as she tried to speak, only to find she couldn't. Apparently he took her parted lips as an invitation. And the moment his mouth covered hers, she wasn't too sure they hadn't been.

His lips were warm, his tongue, when it pushed into her mouth, was firm and hot. She followed his tongue back into his mouth, angling his head to better receive her kiss. He groaned deep in his throat, and suddenly dryness was no longer her problem. Anywhere.

Her skin heated from the inside out, she felt every hair on her body lift as sensation after sensation rippled over her. Her moan answered his as he took command of the kiss, deepening it, expanding it.

The arm under her legs slowly pulled away, but he caught her to his chest and let her slide down his body.

She moved closer to him, wanting to feel his contours mold to hers, wanting to know where he was hard and if it would feel as good as she expected pressed against where she was soft.

Her movements elicited another groan from Zach which vibrated against her mouth. He shifted, dragging her more tightly into his embrace. And she found his hardest place.

And when he moved against her, it was more than good, it was enthralling.

Zach settled her feet more firmly on the ground and slid his hands to the front of her shirt, never once taking his mouth from some part of her body. His fingers worked her buttons as his lips worked her neck. His hands pulled her open shirt from her shorts as his teeth pulled and sucked on her earlobe.

She gasped at the first tentative brush of his fingers against her nipples, then arched into his hand, wanting, needing full contact. He complied immediately.

His kisses moved slowly back to her mouth, taking a long, lingering taste that sent any practical thoughts she had left spinning away.

"I want to taste you, Dara." He pushed her sleeves down to her elbows, forcing her hands to drop from his shoulders. Next came her bra straps, but the sports design wasn't conducive to a trailside tryst. Dara groaned in frustration, but Zach simply stripped her shirt off.

"Take off your bra for me."

His voice was rough, but the look in his eyes was so powerful, her hands completed the task with no direction from her mind. The air was cooler in the trees, but that wasn't why she shivered. Lord, the way he looked at her.

No one had ever looked at her like he did. With such naked want, such need, such intent.

Zach was finding it next to impossible to keep from just pushing her up against the nearest tree, pulling her legs up around his hips and taking her right then and there. God knew he was long past ready. And if the look in her eyes was any indication, so was she.

But he forced himself to slow down, to take each moment for the separate thrill it was. She stood there, her hair wild and mussed, her shorts half open from his fumbled efforts to pull her blouse out. And her breasts. He forced his gaze back to her face and felt as if he'd just taken a running leap off the edge of a cliff. His heart dropped to his knees, the adrenaline sent another hot rush into his system, his pulse roared.

Never would he have thought that the expression in a woman's eyes could be more erotic, more arousing, more totally captivating, than her naked body. But he couldn't look away.

She took one of his hands and placed it on her breast. He shuddered. She moaned and shifted under his hand. In the next instant, he'd cupped her nape and pulled her hard against him, fusing his mouth on hers, pouring all the intensity of what she made him feel into that one kiss.

The rush he felt crashed over him with such strength and power, he thought he might actually come from just touching her, from just kissing her.

Her hand dove into his hair, and she hungrily returned his kiss. He felt her other hand slide down his chest to the button of his jeans. His better judgment warred with primal desire. Judgment won out. A split second before her hand could brush against him, he backed away from her.

Dara stumbled backward a step, her expression a bit wild and unfocused. She wobbled a bit as she bent down to retrieve her shirt, but she was moving away from him before he could reach out to help.

"Dara." His voice was little more than a rough growl. "Look at me."

She slid her arms into her shirt, keeping her back to him.

He curled his fingers into his palm to keep from reaching for her. "Please." Her actions stilled for a split second, then continued. "Don't hide from me, Dart."

With a sigh of disgust, she gave up trying to button her shirt and turned to him. "I'm not—"

"God, you're beautiful." The words just tumbled out, heartfelt, soul-deep. Something deep inside twisted painfully when she automatically reached up and held her shirt closed. "I was looking at you when I said that. Not your open shirt."

He couldn't tell if her cheeks were red from his beard, or from a blush. Stepping forward, he slowly reached for her hair, softly untangling the wild snarls he'd created.

"I have a pretty good idea what you're thinking right now," he said quietly.

"No, you—"

"Shhh. I stopped you because I was about a nanosecond from disgracing myself. If your hand had moved even a quarter of an inch . . ." Now the blush was apparent. He smiled, feeling tender and protective and a whole bunch of things he didn't want to analyze. "And I don't know about you, but I had a different idea in mind for our first time."

He watched her throat work as she swallowed. She started to speak, but stopped, looked away for a moment, then finally back at him. "I guess it's sort of ridiculous to deny there will be a first time at this point?"

She smiled, and Zach laughed softly before growing serious. "Can you honestly say you don't want to?" Zach wasn't sure he was ready for her answer, so he didn't allow her time to give him one. "I know you're keeping some mental list in your head about the pros and cons of our having a relationship."

She stiffened, and Zach stifled the urge to curse.

"One of us has to be sensible."

"And it goes without saying it can't be me, right?" Zach clamped his mouth shut before he said something stupid he'd regret forever. A moment later, he said, "I hate to break it to you, Dara, but we're already having a relationship. Whether you want to or not. As long as we keep spending time together, this will keep happening. And it won't be long before it's a whole lot more than this. You know it and I know it."

"Does it make any difference to you that I wish it wouldn't?"

Bang. Dead center. The intensity of the pain took him totally by surprise. "Why?" The question was nothing more than a hoarse whisper. "Would it really be so awful? Am I such a poor bargain, Dart?"

She lifted shaky fingers and traced them over his mouth. Damn if his eyes didn't burn. Why was this so hard? Why the hell did it matter so much?

"Honestly, Zach? I think the reason I can't seem to

stop this from happening is because a part of me wants it too. A big part. Badly." The last word sounded as if it had been forced from her.

"Then what's the problem?"

"The problem is that for you, this is . . ." She shrugged. "I don't know, for fun, casual. Not serious." She turned away. "I can't explain it."

"And for you it's not? Is that what you're saying?" He pulled her gently back around, keeping his hands on her shoulders. "Dara?"

She looked up at him, and the wariness he saw in her eyes tore at him. "I'm not real good at casual."

"I've never felt less casual about anything in my life."

"Maybe I know that too," she said, so softly, he wasn't sure he heard her correctly. "Maybe that's why I keep making lists. So neither of us gets hurt." She moved a step back. "And I think I'd rather have you as a friend forever, than a, than a . . ."

"A lover, Dara. You can say it. Lovers. And who says we can't have both? Which brings us back to the original question of how we'd have one without the other. You know as well as I do what would have happened if I hadn't stopped just now."

Her eyes darted away, then suddenly her mouth curved in a small smile, then erupted into a soft laugh.

"What's so damn funny?"

"Nothing." She giggled again. "Which is just what would have happened. You said yourself if I'd touched you, you would have—"

"I know what I said!" He turned around, then found himself fighting the urge to laugh too.

Careful to keep his back to her, he said, "I'm trying

to be serious here, Dara." He heard her stifle a snort and spun around. One look and they both burst into laughter. They laughed until they each had to hold on to the nearest tree for support.

Several moments later, he walked to her and pulled her gently into a loose embrace. He released a deep sigh as she looped her arms around his waist and let her head drop forward onto his chest.

He lost track of how long he stood there with her in his arms. He tightened his hold slightly and leaned down to whisper in her ear. "Let it happen, Dara. Let's just let it happen."

Dara didn't say anything, but a few seconds later she stretched up on tiptoe and kissed him gently on his neck. She moved her arms from around his waist and turned away from him.

He let her go, feeling oddly as if a part of him had just gone with her. He stopped short of helping her button her shirt. Just the knowledge that she wasn't wearing a bra any longer would likely keep him in pain the rest of the way up the trail.

He found the bra dangling from a thin tree limb and unsnagged it, giving her plenty of time before he turned back to her.

"You still want to sit down for a while?"

"How much farther is it?"

"About a mile and a half."

She raked her fingers through her hair, doing little to untangle the snarls, but quite a lot to increase Zach's discomfort.

"Might as well get on with it."

His cocky grin finally resurfaced, and he wiggled his

eyebrows suggestively. "I thought that's what we were just doing."

Dara rolled her eyes as she brushed by him. "Get your mind out of the boys' locker room, Brogan."

He started after her. "Hey, I resent that!" he called out. "It's at least in the men's locker room by now."

Dara flashed a smile over her shoulder. "Last one to the top is a rotten egg!" She took off toward the trail, her laughter ringing through the trees.

"Now who's still in grade school, Dart the Dragon Colbourne?" he yelled.

She turned around and stuck her tongue out at him, then squealed when he took off toward her at a dead run.

Leaving her pack behind, she tore up the dirt path, but after the first fifty yards, her blisters screamed in protest. She raised her hands over her head and spun toward him. "I surrender, I—oof!"

Zach barely had time to duck his shoulder and scoop her up in his arms before trotting to a stop.

She braced her hands on his shoulders and looked down at him. They were both laughing between gasping for breath. He let her feet drop lightly to the ground and pulled her to him for a quick, hard kiss.

He groaned and rested his forehead on hers. "Dara, we're going to have to talk about this, you know."

"I thought that was my line." She leaned up and kissed him again before pulling away. "I'm trying, Zach. Okay? But no talk, not yet. Give me a chance to get used to this 'go for it' mentality, first. It's not as easy as it used to be." She didn't wait for his answer, just winked at him and started back down the trail.

Zach stood there watching her walk away and wondered just when his own "go for it" philosophy had changed to "grab hold and don't let go."

Dara studied the small dome-shaped structure Zach had just popped up. "You have the nerve to call that a tent?"

Zach grinned at her. "All the comforts of home."

"If you're Fred Flintstone, maybe."

Zach rolled back on his heels and stood. "Aw, it's not that bad. Besides, all you're going to do is sleep in it."

Dara thought his eyebrows might have lifted with a hint of a question, but she didn't take the bait. She was working hard at not analyzing things, not thinking about her past or all the really good reasons she had for why Zach was the last man on earth for her. But it didn't require much thought to know she wasn't ready to share a tent, much less a sleeping bag with Zach Brogan. Or maybe she was too ready.

She shrugged and smiled with determination. "You have a point." She bent down—way down—and peered inside the small tomblike dome. If she lay flat on her back and reached both arms out, her fingertips would brush the sides. "I guess I can always just change clothes inside my sleeping bag."

"Hey, don't turn yourself into a pretzel on my account."

Dara mimicked his innocent expression, then said, "I managed to change clothes inside my sleeping bag when I was fourteen, I guess I can do it now."

"I thought you said you'd never been camping."

"I haven't. But you've never had your survivalist skills

truly challenged until you've lived through a teenage slumber party."

"Speaking for all fourteen-year-old boys everywhere, I'm sure they'd love to give it a try."

"You could speak for a fourteen-year-old boy."

He pressed a hand against his chest. "Oh, she still scorches the heart." Chuckling, he grabbed for her hand and pulled her down into his lap.

Dara shifted around until she could look at him, causing a reaction she'd have to be dead not to notice.

She was far from dead. Quite the opposite.

"So, why did you change clothes in your sleeping bag?" he asked. "Weren't all the slumberers girls?"

Dara rolled her eyes. "I hope you have many daughters, Zach Brogan. It would be the ultimate justice." She ignored the odd expression that flickered in his eyes, though it caused a strange reaction deep in her belly. "But to answer your question," she went on, "I was spending the night at Mary Beth Waters's house. Mary Beth and her best friend Toni were, shall we say, early bloomers."

Zach grinned, his gaze dropping to the front of her shirt. Only a small part of her wished she'd put her bra back on. A part that was amazingly easy to ignore.

"Well, speaking from, ah, firsthand experience—" Zach ducked and just barely missed her attempt to pull his hair. "Your blooms are quite wonderful, Ms. Colbourne."

His smile faded from cocky to sincere, and Dara felt her cheeks warm. "Why thank you, Mr. Brogan," she said, refusing to let things get serious. "Coming from an expert such as yourself, I'm flattered." Wrong answer, she realized too late.

His smile faded altogether, but she quickly scrambled out of his lap. This line of conversation had gone on long enough. Dara was halfway across the clearing before she realized he was still sitting by the tent.

She turned. "Zach?"

Zach waved. "Right here." Then under his breath he added, "Which is where I'm staying until I think I can stand again." The way she'd torn out of his lap had left serious doubt that he'd be able to fulfill her prophecy of having daughters. Or sons for that matter.

"Come on, you said you'd show me where the kids could go fishing."

Zach groaned. She'd traded her hiking boots for sneakers and Band-Aids back on the trail. Since then she'd fairly hopped up the remaining part of the service road. Gone was the woman who was afraid of heights and terrified of snakes. Except for the comment about the tent he'd provided for her in lieu of the portable condo she'd packed, she'd been all enthusiasm and bounding energy.

In short, he'd created a monster. Dart the Dragon had returned with a vengeance.

EIGHT

Zach slowly rolled to his knees and pushed to a stand. When he was sure he could walk without looking like he'd just spent a month on horseback, he headed her way.

She stood at the edge of the clearing, hands on her hips. The stance pulled at the buttons of her blouse, not letting him ignore the fact that her sports bra was still in his backpack. But he didn't let his gaze linger on the shadowed fullness of her breasts. Instead, as he closed the distance between them, he kept his attention focused on her. All of her. She'd mystified him as a child, provoking him to do idiotic things that had resulted in alienating her. He stopped a few feet away from her, reveling in the discovery that the enchantment was still there. Only far more potent. *Please Lord*, he found himself silently praying, *don't let me do anything stupid to mess things up this time*.

"Which way?"

"The lake is over here." He gestured toward a gently

sloping path that had been recently widened, although he was pleased to see the crew he'd hired had taken pains to keep it from looking that way. The other surrounding paths, as well as the service road they'd hiked up on, had also been recently graded to remove the deep ruts the winter runoff always created. From the looks of it so far, the buggies should do just fine.

"I know I said it all looked the same earlier." Dara shifted her gaze to the sweeping vista spread out below them. The fields in the valley were sectioned off, planted with various crops, making them look like an odd game board, with the small farmhouses and other buildings resembling small playing pieces scattered about haphazardly. "But up here the view is simply outstanding." She turned to face him. "You picked a beautiful spot, Zach."

"I think the kids will like it."

Dara gave him a "we'll see" look. He loved knowing he could drive her to complete distraction in less than five seconds almost as much as he loved the reemerging wildness in her. But he realized he was equally drawn to her business-only side, and he actually liked the way she insisted on analyzing everything. Maybe even when it came to the two of them.

She kept him on his toes, made him look at things from a different perspective, challenging him on levels he'd never experienced. Like one long never-ending thrill ride.

A ride he was rapidly discovering he didn't want to ever end.

"Don't count your parachutes before they've opened, Brogan," she cautioned. "You still have two days' worth of a schedule to sell me on."

"I know they'll like it. Just as I know your report to the board and their parents will get it approved. "I mean, *I* planned it, didn't I?"

She sighed and patted his cheek. "Maybe your body didn't outgrow your ego after all."

He laughed and lunged for her, but she was too quick and dashed several yards down the path.

Zach caught up to her and slipped his hand in hers, liking the way her fingers felt between his. "So," he asked cheerfully, "you ever fish with live bait before?"

An owl screeched in the dark, prompting Dara to tuck in her legs Indian fashion and shift as close to the fire as she dared. "This is really good," she said, scooping up another heaping spoonful of chili.

Zach polished off the last bite. "I guess it's a good thing I brought a few cans."

"If you're going to start again on my fishing skills—"

"What fishing skills?"

Dara picked up a small rock and tossed it at him. It landed square in the middle of his chili, splattering his sweatshirt with red sauce.

Zach looked down in disbelief, then across the fire at her. "Oh, Colbourne, you're gonna pay for that one."

Dara immediately set down her bowl and scrambled to her feet, but Zach was already halfway around the small ring of rocks. She turned and blindly began to run, shrieking as she dodged trees.

"Running won't save you this time, little girl."

"Wanna bet?" Her words were barely audible as she sucked in another lungful of clean night air.

A hand circled her arm and pulled her around in a wide loop until she landed against the hard surface of his body.

"Yeah, I wanna bet."

She smacked him on the chest. "The least you could do"—she paused to catch her breath—"is be a little out of breath." She looped her arms around his waist and rested her forehead on his shirt.

She could feel his heart pounding. The force of it belied his apparent ease in catching her. She smiled against the gray fabric, warmed by his body.

"You do things to my breath," he said softly, "that put scaling Annapurna or K2 to shame."

A little shiver raced over her skin, making her wonder why she'd worked so hard all afternoon to stay out of his reach. It hadn't been easy. They'd gone fishing, trail blazing, discussed Zach's strategies for everything from finding a way for the kids to answer nature's call to making sure they'd be able to take on most of the camp chores themselves.

Zach could have easily pushed it, but he hadn't. She'd been relieved, thinking time would help her put his effect on her in some sort of perspective. But now, in his arms again, she knew no amount of time, short of the rest of her life, would ever dull the impact he had on her.

Her head buzzed at the feel of his hands. Without actually deciding to do it, she lifted her head and licked at a spot of chili sauce. Then another. And another.

She felt his chest flex as she continued her quest.

"Taste good?" His voice was as dark as the night.

"Mmm-hmm," she murmured.

"Makes me wish I'd thought of this when you spilled coffee on your blouse."

Dara's nipples hardened at his whispered suggestion. On impulse, she leaned over and sucked on the nipple barely detailed under his sweatshirt.

His sudden inward breath pulled his chest away from her, but his arms held her tight against him. "Do that again."

She'd started to lift her head away, but the gentle pressure of his hand on the back of her neck was more provocation than she needed. She slowly pulled his other nipple in her mouth until it too could be felt through his sweatshirt. She could hear his breath come even harder. So she did it again.

He groaned. Setting her just slightly away from him, Zach yanked his sweatshirt over his head, then immediately pulled her back to him. Dara lifted her hands to his waist, then drew them slowly over the contours of his hard, flat abdomen, tangling in the soft dark blond hair that whorled across his upper chest.

She licked her lips.

He groaned again, deep in the back of his throat. "Taste me, Dara. Go on."

She parted her lips, slowly sliding her tongue out, then very lightly flicked the soft circle of skin around his nipple. Her gaze drifted upward just as her lips closed around the tightened knot of flesh.

His eyes glittered, looking black and bottomless under the moonlit sky. He pulled her closer, his arm dropping to her waist, then lower, cupping her hips to his. Dara was beyond ready for the feel of the hard length of him. Her knees buckled, but she didn't have time to worry about standing. Zach pulled her head back and lowered his mouth to hers.

Then his tongue drove into her mouth, once, twice, then again and again as his hips moved against her, and both breathing and staying upright ceased to matter. Responding to him, his response to her, that was her sole focus. The force of what he made her feel, of what her own actions made her feel, rocked her hard.

Her hands lifted to his face. She tilted his head as she dueled with his tongue for control of the kiss, reveling in the ferocity of his need for her, but unable to master her need to be fierce as well. So she stopped trying.

She'd worried about being swept away in a storm of passion like she had with Daniel, but she knew this was far more powerful than anything Daniel had inspired in her. Maybe she'd always known that.

Zach let her in, let her taste him. He bent and lifted her up, finally, mercifully pressing himself where she needed to feel him most. And it still wasn't enough. She squirmed in his arms, half wild for him and reveling in the fact that he was equally wild for her.

"Hold on to me," he whispered into her mouth.

Her arms went around his neck, her fingers digging into the dense muscles of his back. She felt them flex and contract as he moved. She pulled his bottom lip into her mouth. She moved to his chin, then along his jaw, the slight abrasion of his shadowed beard against her already tender lips intensifying the sensations rocketing through her.

Suddenly there was a rough surface biting into her back, and she gasped.

She barely had time to register that she was wedged

between his body and a tree before he was pulling her legs up over his hips. And when the rigid length of him was finally centered, he began moving against the ache between her legs, easing it, tormenting it, strengthening it. She cried out against the damp, salty skin of his throat.

"Oh God, Zach." She breathed hard against his neck, as he continued to ride her. "Oh my God." She desperately wanted to make him stop so she could tear her pants off, then his, but that would mean he'd have to move away from her, and she simply couldn't make him do that. Just the thought had her convulsively tightening her thighs on his hips.

Zach framed her face with his hands and brought his mouth down on hers again. This time he controlled it, he tasted and sucked and licked. She gave in to the tight feeling that was snaking its way up her belly, swelling her breasts, tightening her nipples, making her sweat. He rubbed his flat palm over her nipple until it hardened to a small, hot ache. His mouth trailed from hers. He nipped at her chin, then traced his tongue down her throat. He tormented her the way she'd tormented him until she wanted to claw her shirt off, desperate to feel his mouth, tongue, and teeth on her bare skin.

And still he rode her, his hips never slowing, never stopping their primal rhythm.

"Don't stop," she whispered, barely able to form the words. "Zach. Zach. Oh . . . my . . . God. Zach!"

The third time his name rushed in a high shriek as the coil whiplashed back down her body and snapped hard between her legs.

"I'm here, baby. I'm here." He whispered her name

over and over; against her breast, on her throat, along her jaw, and finally into her mouth.

She felt him shudder against her, his hips bucking hard and staying tight. He gathered her in his arms, turned and slid slowly down the trunk of the tree until they were sitting in a sprawl of arms and legs at its base.

He kissed her long and deep, his arms tight around her. She held him tightly, too, almost afraid if she didn't, they'd both implode from the force of what had just taken place. His kisses gentled then, soft, sweet kisses that made her eyes burn, until finally he stopped, leaving his lips on hers.

"Can you reach my feet?"

His words vibrated against her lips. His mouth left hers and rested in the crook of her neck.

She wound her fingers in his hair and held him there. "What?" She knew he'd said something, but the words were so incongruous, her mind refused to interpret them.

"My feet. I want you to uncurl my toes."

"Oh." She smiled against his hair.

Slowly the world around them came back into focus. The night breeze, the sounds of the crickets, the frogs, and Lord knew what other slithery mountain creatures, the black sky studded with more stars than she'd thought existed.

"Dart, I'm—"

She gripped his head closer against her neck. "Shh."

He pulled from her grasp and looked at her. For a long moment they stared at each other, then Zach leaned back against the tree, arranging her sideways in his lap, tucking her against his chest, his arms tight around her.

"It's funny," he said.

She looked up at him. "Funny?"

"Maybe ironic is a better word." Before she could ask, he continued. "I'm thirty. I've been with women. Seen lots of breasts. I've even had some pretty spectacular climaxes."

Dara started to pull from his arms, but they hardened, like prison bars. "Zach, I don't—"

"But you will. This time. Now."

"I don't want to hear this," she said.

"Yes, you do. Trust me." It wasn't a question. But when he tilted her head up to his, the question was there in his eyes. "I need you to understand."

She couldn't look away from him. She'd never seen him like this. She'd seen shades of this side of him that first day in her office, and there had been one or two glimpses since. But she really hadn't thought he was capable of being this intense, this . . . serious. She dipped her chin in the slightest of nods, still not really wanting to hear the rest, but willing to. For him.

"I wasn't trying to be crude. But it was necessary to make my point."

"Which is?"

"Which is that because I've done so many wild things, both personally and professionally, I guess I'd sort of gotten a little smug. Only I didn't realize it."

"Smug?" Her grin came out of nowhere, and she clung to it, feeling normal with him for the first time since he'd caught her when she'd run.

"Smug," he repeated. "Oh, I enjoyed myself. Made sure it was mutual. I was smart, made sure I was safe, that my partner was safe. And figured that was as good as it got. And for the most part, it was pretty damn good."

Dara looked away. She didn't know which was worse, the idea of another woman getting pleasure in his arms, or that she was likely just another name on that list.

"And now?" She forced the words out.

He took her face in his hands, daring her to look at him again. His eyes never left hers. "And now I realize I didn't have a clue."

Zach lowered his mouth to within a heartbeat of hers. "What just happened between you and me, against this tree . . . It was wild and hot and out of control. And it should have just been great sex. We didn't even take our pants off. I wasn't inside you." He visibly swallowed. "But it had nothing to do with sex, did it? God help me, Dart, but I don't think I've ever felt like I was deeper inside another person in my whole life."

His kiss was gentle yet insistent. She kissed him back, hoping it was what he needed, hoping that when she looked at him again, that awful emptiness would be gone. Not daring to think about what she needed or wanted.

He didn't let her see. He simply pulled her head back to his chest. She felt his cheek come to rest on her hair.

For several long minutes, she just sat there, concentrating on her heartbeat. And his. She felt completely unprepared. And nervous. And big-time scared.

"You said it was ironic," she reflected, no longer able to bear the silence of her own thoughts.

He sighed, but the small chuckle she felt more than heard reassured her. "Being around you, with you . . . I don't know. I've never felt like this. And I seem to have this compulsion to discuss it with you." He pressed a kiss to her hair. "Which is natural, since, after all, you're the champion analyzer of this pair."

She smiled, and her muscles relaxed just a little. "And now I'm the one who doesn't want to talk."

"Yeah. Figures, doesn't it?"

Dara sat up, holding on to his shoulders for support. She looked straight at him. "Zach, I'm not sure what you want from me."

"I'm not sure what you want from me, either, Dara. Maybe that's what's scaring the hell out of me."

"You're scared too?" She didn't realize what she'd revealed until it was too late.

"Out of my ever-loving mind."

It should have made her feel better. And maybe, in some crazy way, it did. "What are we going to do about it?"

"Follow our instincts?" He winked. "They've led us down some pretty interesting paths so far, wouldn't you say?"

Her smile was more tentative. "I keep wanting to be smart about this. I had to make some pretty hard choices a while back." She looked down for a moment, then back up at him. "And until now, I thought I was clear on what was best for me. I honestly don't know if that's you. And yet . . ." She ended on a whisper. "I can't seem to stop myself."

"Me either." He dropped a quick kiss on her nose, then another on her mouth. "I know you have reasons for the choices you've made, Dara. Just as I know we're different. But different doesn't have to mean incompatible."

She laughed, the hoarse sound surprising them both. "Oh, I think our compatibility is more than fine."

Zach laughed too. "Yeah, well, if all we ever do is make love then we'll be okay."

Dara's breath caught, and Zach's gaze swung to hers. Her lips parted, and he leaned in closer.

"I want more than that," she whispered.

"Yeah, I know," he whispered back. "So do I." He nipped at her lips. "So do I." Then his mouth took hers and there were no more words.

Zach felt his body tighten again. She was returning his kiss, and he didn't want to stop. But he knew this time it wouldn't end up with them half dressed, or dressed at all. And it's not how he wanted them to take the next step. This wasn't even close to how he'd planned to take the first one.

He pulled his mouth from hers and gently shifted her from his lap. Standing a bit awkwardly, he reached down and pulled her up into an easy embrace. "I think I'd, um, better go and clean up."

She smiled even as she blushed. "Yeah." She stepped out of his arms and turned back toward camp.

He tucked her hand in his as he walked next to her. "You want to go with me?"

She looked at him, her expression unreadable. "I . . . no. No, I'm all right."

She dropped his hand as soon as they were close to their campsite, and Zach dragged his duffel bag out of his tent. He gathered a few things and turned to ask Dara a question, but was greeted by the lovely sight of her derriere poking up in the air as she rooted around in her own tent.

"No," he instructed himself under his breath. "Go wash up." Then he chuckled.

"What's so funny?" She turned and sat with her arms crossed over her bent knees.

"I think I just told myself to go jump in a lake."

"Huh?"

He grinned. "You sure you don't want to come with me?"

Her frown changed to a knowing smile. "Zach," she said sweetly, "go jump in the lake."

He was still chuckling as he grabbed his duffel bag and headed down the trail they'd taken earlier that afternoon to go fishing.

Dara watched him go, coming very close to grabbing her own gear and running to catch up with him. "No," she told herself, "you've played with his fire enough tonight."

She smiled and looked over at their real fire, which was now a pile of glowing embers. She headed over to their small stash of edibles and eating utensils. It only took a few minutes to find the marshmallows. "Drat. No skewers." She glanced around. "Sticks. I need sticks."

She started for the small stand of trees, then noticed the remainders of their dinner—such as it was. "Shoot. Those plates will never come clean now." Zach had filled a collapsible jug with water from a nearby spring, but she hated to waste it soaking off the hardened chili.

There was, however, a whole lake's worth of water not two hundred yards away.

After scraping off the worst of it, she stuffed the bowls, spoons, and small cooking pot in the zippered mesh sack Zach had brought. She stopped long enough to wrap a fresh shirt and jeans in a towel, and grab a flashlight before setting off for the lake. Surely, Zach would be finished by the time she got there.

She was about fifty yards away from the water when she heard the music. It was so surprising, she stopped for a moment to listen.

She laughed and closed the remaining distance. As she rounded the last turn, she shouted, "Yo, wild thing, you decent?"

"Yo, wild thing?"

Dara stumbled at the sound of his voice. It was much closer than she'd expected. A second later Zach stepped from the trees to her right, bare-chested and tugging his zipper up.

She wanted to tug it right back down again. Instead she lifted the mesh bag. "A cavewoman's job is never done. I just wanted to make sure you were through with the tub before I used it as a sink."

Zach lifted the bag from her hands. "Why didn't you just use the water in camp?"

"It'll take a while for this to soften up, and I didn't want to make you lug more water back from the spring."

"Well, why don't I toss this in and tie it to a bush while you take a bath?" He laughed. "Gee, doesn't this have a *Twilight Zone* sort of domestic ring to it?"

Dara laughed with him. "I'm not sure I can bathe to The Troggs. You wouldn't happen to have anything a little less, you know—"

"Earthy?" He stepped closer. "Primal?"

The gleam in his eyes made her step back. "Never mind. I'll bathe to the frog and cricket chorus."

"You want me to wait for you?"

Dara was tempted to say the hell with it and ask him to join her. "No. I'm just going to rinse off. The water up here is a bit cold for a moonlight swim."

"Keep your flashlight on. Just set it on a rock with the beam upward, like a beacon."

"You got it."

He turned away, and she thought she heard him say, "Yeah, really, really bad." But when he looked over his shoulder, he said, "If you're not back in fifteen, I'm coming after you."

Dara waved and turned to the lake. His autocratic command should have rankled, but it didn't. His concern was completely different than the way Dane looked out for her. Different and sort of nice. She could get to liking that kind of concern. The music drifted off as he made his way back to camp, and Dara quickly shed her clothes.

Of course, she thought wickedly, *just because I like it doesn't mean I can't stay here for eighteen minutes just to get a rise from him.*

She shivered, and it had nothing to do with the cool mountain air and everything to do with the knowledge that she'd already gotten quite a rise out of him.

She could get to liking that too.

Dara had just slipped a loose-knit sweater over her head when the soft strains of music drifted to her. She bent to roll up her dirty clothes in her towel and run a quick comb through her hair. By the time she straightened, the music had grown loud enough for her to make out the song.

Zach stepped into the clearing and set his small portable boom box on a rock. He walked over to her, took the clothes roll from her hands and set that down too.

He pulled her into his arms. "Dance with me?"

Art Garfunkel sang "I Only Have Eyes For You" into the night, and Dara was swaying even before her arms closed around his neck. She laid her head on his chest. "I thought you were supposed to sing around the campfire."

"I'm not a very good singer."

She looked up and smiled. "You admit to not doing something well?"

He pulled her head back to his chest. "Shut up and dance."

She continued to rock slowly back and forth. "I'm not sure this will be a good substitute for the kids," she said, long moments later, her words getting softer as the music and the feel of Zach in her arms worked their magic.

"Scotty can sing with the kids. He's great."

He pulled her hips closer to his, and Dara swallowed a moan. "So, this isn't part of the scheduled trip then?"

"No," he whispered roughly, "this is because I couldn't stand not having you in my arms again tonight."

NINE

Dara slipped her arms from his neck and wrapped them around his waist. Hugging him as tightly as he hugged her, she gave up all pretense of talk and just let Zach and the music invade her body and soul.

The last strains of the song echoed out over the water, and Zach halted their dance. Lifting her chin up, he lowered his head very slowly.

"It's true, you know."

"What's true?" she whispered, barely able to form the words for wanting his mouth on hers.

"The song. It's a beautiful star-filled, moonlit night. And I can't take my eyes off you."

Dara couldn't wait. She lifted on tiptoe and closed the distance between her lips and his. He held back just enough that she slid her arms from his waist and pulled his head down. She poured everything she felt into that kiss; her desire for him, her growing need to be with him all the time, her fear that this was wrong, her apprehension that in the end it was going to be more painful than she could stand.

Whether because Zach sensed her turmoil, or was simply feeling it, too, he pulled away and rested his forehead on hers before it got out of control.

For a long moment, the only sound was that of their shallow breathing. Then Zach said, "You okay?"

After a slight pause, she answered. "No. You?"

He pulled her into a fierce hug which she returned. "I can't decide what I am right now."

Dara knew they needed some space, and some time. Funny, she'd never have thought the great outdoors could be so incredibly intimate.

The thought brought a much-needed smile to her face and the strength to step out of his arms. "You hungry?"

Zach groaned. "Bad double entendre, Dart."

She turned and grabbed her towel roll as Zach stepped over and snagged the mesh net from the bush and scooped up the boom box.

"There is one camping tradition we haven't yet observed," she said.

His grin was wide and lazy. "Sleeping naked under the stars?"

"Gee," she said, "I must have missed that one."

"Shame, shame. And you said your research was thorough."

"It's your research that has to be thorough. I'm not here as the camping expert." Her gaze narrowed as his grin widened. "No wisecracks, Brogan."

"Who me?" He looked wounded. She didn't buy it for a second. "And here I was going to tell you how impressed I've been with your adaptation to mountain life."

Dara's laugh was more a derisive snort. "Yeah, I bet this has been one thrill-seeking minute after another for someone like you."

Zach's grin faded. He stepped closer to her, the bowls in the mesh bag clinking together. "Someone like me?"

Dara would have looked away, but something in his expression stopped her.

"What do you think of me, Dara? Honestly." He lifted his free hand to her hair, smoothing the wispy tendrils back from her face. "Never mind. I already know."

"How could you know, I've—"

"I catch you looking at me occasionally." A small smile curved his mouth, more wistful than cocky. "Sometimes they're the sort of looks that make me want to beat my chest and start removing clothes without unbuttoning them first."

Dara felt her cheeks heat.

"And then there are the other ones. The ones that say, 'What am I doing with this Neanderthal?' The ones that wonder how you can be attracted to a guy who cruises the globe in search of the next adrenaline high instead of growing up, finding a respectable job and making a real contribution to society."

Dara was already shaking her head before he'd finished, but Zach either didn't notice or didn't care. He traced his fingertips across her lips and let his hand fall away.

"Zach—"

"Don't, Dara." He smiled, and the brightness of his

white teeth glowing at her in the moonlight when his eyes looked so deep and fathomless made Dara's eyes burn. "I remember Dane telling me once that after he'd regaled you with war stories from our latest annual trip—I think it was four or five years ago, when we did the Amazon thing—"

"That 'Amazon thing' consisted of trekking down a part of the river not even the local tribesmen will go near, or so Dane told me, just to go fishing."

"Peacock bass are considered a major trophy," he said, his tone reverent.

She rolled her eyes. "It was crazy and foolish and could have gotten all three of you in serious trouble." Dara pulled away from his disquieting touch.

"I seem to recall Dane saying that you thought I should be locked up as a threat to civilized society."

"I can tell you find that incredibly insulting."

Zach's grin was more natural this time. "No. Society is entirely too civilized as it is. My clients understand that." He assumed a dignified expression. "Hence my popularity." She giggled and without warning, he dipped his head down and caught her mouth in a short, fierce kiss.

Dara responded instantly. It was over before she could think straight.

"What's insulting," he said softly, "is that you don't trust your instincts more. Your head isn't empty and neither is mine. This isn't about hormones, Dara. Look below the surface. I dare you. Or is that what scares you?" His gaze searched hers in a way that made her feel naked and vulnerable. "You afraid you might find something worth being interested in? Or that you won't?" He cupped her face and dropped his lips to hers again. "And how would you rationalize the fact that you want me so bad, you can taste it," he said roughly, "when I don't come even close to meeting your standards of what's worthy?"

"Zach—"

She wasn't given the chance to explain or defend herself, not that she had even the remotest idea what she would have said.

She watched him head down the path back to camp. A few seconds later, he called out. "Turn your flashlight on." He paused until she aimed her beam at the trees to his right, then disappeared into the darkness just beyond the circle of light.

Zach found the bag of marshmallows next to the water jug. Dara's camping tradition. He swore under his breath. What the *hell* had he been thinking back there? Pushing her like that?

He shook his head and grabbed the plastic bag. Daring her, challenging her, that's what he'd been doing.

"And just what the hell did you hope to accomplish?" he asked himself as he foraged around the edge of the campsite for a few sticks. He couldn't quite erase the image of her eyes, all wide and hurt. But he knew Dara, and the hurt wouldn't last long. Oh no, anger should kick in any old time now. He half expected her to come busting back into the clearing and give him a well-ordered piece of her mind, to tell him he was wrong about her, tell him that she—

That she what? What was he trying to prove here?

That he could win her over despite her very good reasons for not getting involved? And then what? If she fell in love with him—

Zach froze in the act of scooping up another stick, the knot in his chest tightened to the point of pain. Love him? Is that what he really wanted? Wanting him, needing him enough to be with him, that wasn't enough?

No. The answer was instant and as clear in his mind as the midnight sky. No. He wanted it all. He wanted her today, tomorrow, and all the rest of his days. He wanted her smiles, her moods, her laughter, her arguments, her kisses, her touches, her predictable reactions to his teasing, and the outrageous responses he never saw coming. Dear Lord, he wanted her always.

And along with that moment of understanding Zach experienced a fear of the type he'd never known before. He'd conquered each and every goal he'd ever set for himself. Sheer grit and determination had always been enough. But it had always been him against nature, the elements, geography. Never a person. Never a woman. Never Dara.

How in the hell was he going to win this time? And when had the stakes ever been so high? The stick snapped in his hands, and he absently tossed the pieces on the glowing embers of the fire. He stared into the small clumps of glowing ash, watching the orange-yellow aura expand and pop as the wood slowly turned to smoke. He identified strongly, feeling as if his own grasp on Dara and their relationship was just as tenuous and intangible.

She thought he was irresponsible, that he traipsed the globe like a wild man, living for the moment, no plans for the future, not caring if he even lived long enough to have one.

Anger rose within him as he jammed a puffy marshmallow onto another stick and lowered it as close to the heat as he dared. He'd always seen himself as a smart man who'd capitalized on his strengths, a successful businessman lucky enough to make a living doing what he loved to do, what he did best. And he made a damn good living.

He dropped down into a crouch, staring into the fire. Anger was replaced by the bleak realization that nothing was the same, the checks and balances of his life, their respective worth had all changed. And Dara was still right. What did he have to offer someone like her? No matter how in touch she got with the girl she'd been, she'd also really and truly changed. And it was a sure bet she wouldn't want to climb mountains, or scale glaciers, or leap from airplanes.

The painful irony was, he didn't care if she did any of those things with him. When he thought of them together, it was doing regular things; grocery shopping on Saturday morning and him sneaking junk food in the cart; watching her stand in front of the closet, picking out the perfect dress so he could show her off on the dance floor that night, having her pull it on so he could pull it right back off again and to hell with going out. He saw fires in winter and barbecues in summer, dinners by candlelight and making love to her on rainy mornings.

He wanted to be there when the emotional fallout from her job was too much to bear alone. He wanted her to be there when he returned from a trip all weary and aching and needing her soft touches and special brand of fierce love.

Her love. That's what it all came back to.

He shook his head, a harsh sigh escaping his lips. And if he told her any of this, she'd laugh herself silly. She'd never believe it. And he couldn't blame her.

The marshmallow, now all black and burned, oozed off the slender stick and plopped into the fire with a loud hiss.

"I see this is another skill you haven't mastered."

Zach jerked his head up. She was standing on the other side of the fire.

"Can't sing camp songs or cook marshmallows. And is afraid of women drivers. Better be careful, Brogan, or they'll revoke your thrill-seeker's license."

He should be glad she was teasing him, that she was trying to make it all right. But the dark shadows of night didn't hide the tight lines of tension on her face, nor did the crackle of the fire cover the underlying strain in her voice. He wasn't glad. He was angry. At her for not rightfully telling him to go to hell and at himself for being so damn glad she hadn't.

He stood up, tossed the stick in the fire and walked around the stones, stopping just in front of her.

"I'm sorry."

"There's a whole bag left," she said, her bright tone faltering on the last word.

"You know what I mean," he said quietly. "I shouldn't have said those things back there. And I shouldn't have walked away."

"I'm a big girl, Zach," she said, her hushed tone making the hair on his arms prickle in awareness. "I can take care of myself."

Zach winced. "Yeah. I guess I ought to get used to that." Her expression was unreadable and after a long silent moment when he didn't have the first clue what to say or do next, he finally gestured behind him. "Would you like a marshmallow? I'll let you cook this time."

"No," she whispered. "I don't want a marshmallow." She stepped closer to him. "And I don't want to sing camp songs." Another small step. She tilted her head to look up at him. "And I don't want to dance." Her hand pressed lightly on his chest, and his breathing came to an abrupt halt. "But most of all," she said so quietly, he barely heard her over the pounding rush in his ears, "most of all, I don't want to fight with you anymore."

She tilted up on tiptoe and pressed a soft kiss to his mouth. It took everything he had to harness the overwhelming need to drag her into his arms and hang on for dear life.

"Dara," he said, his voice barely a rasp against her lips. "Dart—"

She opened her mouth slightly and kissed him again, taking advantage of his parted lips. He groaned, a shudder of need rocking him so badly, he held on to her hips to steady himself.

"We need to talk," he said, using superhuman effort he hadn't thought himself capable of in order to keep from responding to her. The hard ache between his legs throbbed, reminding him there were some things even his steel will couldn't control. "Dara, please." He lifted his head and framed her face with his hands. "We can't do this until we figure a few things out first." His breath was coming in short, deep pants. "You were right. I'm not . . . maybe you shouldn't . . . not with me." God, why was this so damn hard to say?

"Yeah," she whispered. "I should. And especially with you."

"Why?" he demanded, feeling equal parts confusion and frustration. "You know what I'm like. You said you knew this was wrong. That you'd get hurt."

He dropped his hands to his sides, lowered his gaze and took a deep breath, then looked back into her eyes. "I want you, Dara. More than I could have ever imagined wanting someone. But even more, I don't want to hurt you."

"I stood back there by the lake and had a long talk with myself. And I came to a few inescapable conclusions."

"Such as?"

Her lips curved ever so slightly, and Zach felt his stomach drop to his knees. "I know you, Zach Brogan. I know what you are is more than just what you do." She paused for an unsteady breath. "And I know that in order to experience the joy I could have with you, I have to risk the pain." She reached up and pulled his head down to hers. "And I know I need you badly enough to take that risk again." She kissed him hard and long, and somehow he managed to keep his hands at his sides.

She lifted her mouth from his and looked him straight in the eyes. "There. Now we've discussed it. So, please, Zach, kiss me back." Her voice dropped to a dark, husky whisper. "And this time, don't stop."

Had her expression faltered even once, had he detected even a glimmer of indecision, Zach told himself he might have been able to resist. But all he found when he looked in her eyes was passion, and need, and the tiniest trace of vulnerability. It was that glimpse of her unprotected heart that touched a chord deep within him. He was feeling the very same thing, and knew that if pain was a result of what was about to happen, he would likely share in it equally.

But his hands were on her hips, skimming the sides of her breasts, gently squeezing her shoulders then diving into her hair as he angled her mouth for his. And the instant his lips touched hers she groaned, her slender frame vibrating with the depth and force of it. And that easily, all his inner battles, the possible reprisals and any future regrets simply vanished.

He wrapped her in his arms, fitting her soft curves snugly against his chest and hips. He immediately took the kiss as deep as he knew how, expressing the only way he could all the emotions in his head and heart. His tongue took her mouth, as his hands felt her, his hips cradling hers, and he rocked her, carrying her away with him.

And then even that wasn't enough. He wanted to feel her skin. And he wanted friction; hot, steaming, pulsating friction. He wanted to feel her slide over his bare chest, he wanted to feel her long, smooth legs tangled with his, he wanted her fingers stroking him, he wanted his inside her.

He grabbed her hips and pulled her a few inches off the ground. "Wrap your legs around my hips," he commanded against the damp pulse in her throat. She did, and when he felt her softness press against the front of his jeans, he almost lost it again. His groan was long and rough, as he licked her neck, nipped at the soft spot just beneath her ear.

She bent her head and pulled his earlobe between her teeth and sucked. His breath escaped from clenched teeth. He lifted his head, focusing on a tree behind her, and was moving toward it before he'd even consciously made the decision. The act of walking rubbed her against him in the most delicious, mind-numbing way, and for an instant he thought he might have to lay her down on the ground and rip the clothes from their bodies.

"Lord, I ache, Zach."

He'd never get them undressed in time. And that damn tree was at least a hundred miles away.

Her legs tightened around his waist. She rocked against him.

He grunted and rocked harder against her, his need for her too primal to control. "Dear God, Dara. Stop. Stop it." Even as he begged her, he trailed sucking, biting kisses down the side of her neck, pulling at her shirt with his teeth, shifting her up so he could capture the hard nipple pressing against the soft cotton in his mouth.

She moaned and arched her back, offering herself to him so openly, it nearly brought them both to their knees. He staggered to a halt, continuing his erotic foray across the front of her shirt until he'd soaked the other side with his mouth and tongue.

She writhed in his arms. "Let me down, Zach. I'm getting dizzy." She gasped when he pressed her hips down against him. "Oh, God. I can't take . . . much more . . . of this." He pulled her up and pressed her down again, this time letting her feet drop to the ground. "Don't stop now."

A short gust of laughter at her conflicting demands forced its way out of his laboring lungs. He pulled her to him and kissed her deeply again, then held her against him with one arm when her knees wobbled. He wove his fingers into the hair brushing the nape of her neck and tilted her head back.

"You're really sure about this." It wasn't a question, and Zach didn't expect her to answer. He had the answer he needed just by looking in her eyes.

"No tree, Dara. Not on the cold ground." He grinned, feeling suddenly strong, invincible and immortal in a way that even free-falling from the moon couldn't match. "And definitely not with my pants on."

She was breathing heavily, and her laughter was a cross between a choke and a sob. "Yeah," she managed.

He swung her up in his arms and turned toward the two small canvas domes. "Your cave or mine, Wilma?"

She looked at the tents, a small frown creasing the skin between her eyebrows. "Did you, ah, bring any . . . ?" The most erotic blush he'd ever seen colored her moonlit skin.

He grinned. "Any what?"

She punched him on the shoulder. "You know."

He walked to the nearest tent, finding that even the pain due to the new fit of his jeans was a sweet ache. "Yeah, I know. And before you nail me with another right hook, yes, I did."

Her smile nearly made him drop her. It gave a whole new meaning to the term wanton. "Then your cave it is, Fred."

Zach grinned, then tossed his head back and howled at the moon. Dara's sweet laughter filled the night air, prompting Zach to lift her shoulder height and bury his face in her stomach, nuzzling her. She shrieked, still laughing until his head dipped down just below her belly button. The sound strangled in her throat, and she clutched fistfuls of his hair in her hands.

"Zach, what are you—? Oh God."

Zach lifted his head and dropped a swift kiss on her parted lips before kneeling down with her in his lap, his back to the tent entrance.

He kissed her again. "Lady, you are one hell of a sweet, mind-blowing thrill."

Zach scooted backward through the small opening until he was in the center of his sleeping bag. He pulled his shirt off, then he pulled her on top of him.

Straddling his hips, Dara let her gaze drift over Zach's bare chest and up to his face. The circle of woven mesh fabric sewn into the peak of the dome bathed them in soft silvery moonlight.

"Only you would have a tent with a moon roof."

Somehow the shared laughter right in the middle of such exquisite sexual tension only increased her need for him. It was as hot and wild as she'd imagined, but with Zach the intimacy was teasing and fun, filled with a sexy sort of playfulness that was all the more powerful for how open and uninhibited it made her feel.

Zach's brand of lovemaking was as free and unique as the man himself. In the small confines of the tent, Dara felt as if she were soaring high above the ground.

She reached for the button of his jeans.

Zach groaned, his hips lifting automatically against her. "Better be careful, you're playing with dynamite there, sweetheart."

Dara laughed and tugged his zipper down. "Mmm-hmm." She slid her hands into his pants, not in the least surprised that he wasn't wearing anything else. She looked up at him through half-closed eyes.

Zach gasped as her hand closed around him.

His eyes narrowed as she lowered her head, but his wicked grin was way past daring. "Careful, that could blow at any minute."

"Just what are you referring to sir?" she asked, her voice sultry and amused.

With a burst of choked laughter, Zach reached for her hips and swiftly reversed their positions. He pulled her under him and lifted one knee between her thighs, then slowly pressed upward, flexing his thigh again and again until she was moaning.

He pressed his face against her neck, nibbling, sucking and licking. "Teach you to play with explosives."

"Teach me," she gasped.

Zach was past needing to be asked. He toed off his shoes, shoved his pants down and off, then straddled her thighs. Bending low over her, he began to unbutton her blouse, placing kisses on her soft skin as he bared it. The blouse disappeared, and Zach was torn between continuing downward, or languishing for a while. She arched her back under his heated gaze, and the decision was made.

He ran his flat palms over her nipples until they tightened and his mouth savored each one at great and delicious length.

Her back bowed beneath him, her strong hands alternately holding his head to her breasts and clutching at the sleeping bag beneath her.

"Zach . . . please."

"Please what?" he mumbled against the damp skin of her stomach.

"Please stop torturing me."

He looked up, his chin resting on her navel. "Torture? And here I thought I was making you delirious with pleasure."

Dara's laugh was more a sigh of disbelief. "Trade places and I could have you begging for mercy inside of five minutes."

"Begging sounds good." He pulled her pants off swiftly, making her gasp as the cool night air brushed her skin. "But I plan on being inside you for a whole lot longer than five minutes."

"Zach . . ."

He grinned up at her. "Tsk, tsk. Naughty girl, not wearing any underwear. Imagine the sort of things that could lead a guy to believe."

"Oh," she panted, moaning as his mouth found her inner thigh. "I'm way past imagining."

Dara knew the only way she was going to get what she wanted was to take it. Which she reached down and did.

Zach sucked in a deep breath, then released it on a shaky moan. "God, I love it when you get right to the point."

"It's going to end one way or the other," she said, hardly believing she could possibly be having this much fun while being more turned on than she'd ever been in her life. "Personally, I know where I'd like this to be," she said, her hand circling him, "but it's your choice."

In response, Zach grabbed her hands, stretched up over her, bracing his hands on hers, and, beginning with his thighs, slowly pressed his full weight against her. He was reaching past her head for his duffel bag, then almost forgot what he was looking for when she hooked her legs behind his calves and lifted her hips.

"Yes," he said, both to her and in response to the small box he'd finally uncovered. "Your treat or mine?" he said hoarsely. She kept rotating her hips under him, making the decision for him.

His hands were shaking so hard, he could barely tear the packet open, then swore under his breath at having to lift away from her for the few seconds it took to roll it on.

Her heels crossed behind his back before he'd even balanced himself over her, and he was sheathed deep inside her before he knew what hit him. The tight, hot strength of her slender body held him motionless for one long, incredible second after another.

"Zach," she said, her voice husky with want, "move. Move inside of me."

He did, starting long and slow, until her moans became cries and her cries became soft little gasps. By then he'd taken her hips in his hands and was moving deep and hard and fast, Dara matching him stroke for stroke.

He didn't want it to end. Like an everlasting dive off the world's highest cliff. He didn't ever want to hit bottom.

He rocked back on his heels, dragging Dara with him, keeping her legs locked around his waist. The moonlight played exotic nocturnal games with her skin and her eyes.

He suddenly knew exactly how this was going to end. This time. This first, perfect, unforgettable time.

He slid one hand to the small of her back, bracing her

against him, then slid the other one down between her legs to where they were joined. He caressed, stroked, and taunted until she went wild.

"Yeah, Dara, that's it. Go crazy on me. Lose it." She started to buck against him, and he had to grit his teeth not to lose it himself. But he held on, needing to last long enough to witness what he wanted more than his next breath. "Yeah, that's right," he said as her gasps became little screams. "Look at me!" Her eyes flew open just as she convulsed around the aching length of him. "Now. Just . . . let . . . it . . . go!"

And she did. Zach reached for her and pulled her up to straddle his lap, holding her hips while she arched back, thrusting her small breasts forward into his waiting mouth. She was still convulsing around him when he came in a pounding, crashing fury.

TEN

Dara wrapped her arms around Zach, burying her face in the curve of his neck. Zach's arms were like a straitjacket binding her to him, his face pressed against her neck.

Sound was the first sense she fully recovered, and she realized that they were both gasping and panting for breath like they'd just escaped the hounds of hell. For some perverse reason that made her want to laugh. She hugged him tighter as the first giggle escaped her lips.

Zach pulled back. "What, may I ask"—he paused for another deep breath—"is so funny?"

She smiled up at him, wondering what wonderful thing she'd done to deserve this moment. "Well, you were right again."

"Not surprising. Ow!" Zach smiled and rubbed the nose she'd just tweaked. "What omniscient prediction did I make this time?"

"Well, this was certainly . . . explosive."

Zach's laughter joined hers as he leaned forward to lay her back on the sleeping bag, then scooted away.

Dara leaned up on one elbow, openly admiring how graceful and at ease he was in his own body. His beautifully naked body. "Where are you going?"

"To clean up." Her disappointment must have shown. A hot grin slashed his features as he leaned back down and kissed her long and hard. He groped around for something next to her head.

"Here," he said, pushing a small box into her hands. "Hold on to these." He rolled off her and winked at her just before ducking out the door. "We're going to need all of them."

"You underestimate me, Brogan," she yelled after him, but he was gone. She knew as she lay there, that Zach Brogan was the last man she should have fallen in love with, but somehow she'd managed to do it anyway.

Sometime around dawn, Zach lifted his head from her stomach. He reached across her and peered inside the small box.

"Damn. Only three left."

Dara giggled and groaned at the same time.

He kissed her navel. "You want to explain that?"

"No. I think I went numb about an hour ago."

He looked up at her, eyes gleaming. "Great. Then you won't mind if I do this." He leaned up and captured the tip of her breast in his mouth.

She gasped and involuntarily arched against him, her body long since acclimated to his demands. She lifted her head enough to stare into his smiling face. "Have mercy, okay." She dropped her head back when he ignored what she'd said and reached for her other breast. "I hate it when you gloat."

Zach laughed and laid his head back on her belly, listening to the pulsing sounds of her body. Her heartbeat steadied into a regular rhythm, and he purposely let his mind drift, his hand cupping the soft swell of her stomach below his cheek. The resting place seemed comfortable and strangely natural.

Out of nowhere came the image of her stomach swollen with child. His child. He teased himself with the idea of what it would feel like to lie like this and hear two hearts beating beneath his cheek. His body's instinctive response to that brief image was so instant and overwhelming, he had to shift positions.

Dara's hand came to rest on his head, and she stroked a wild tangle of hair from his cheek.

"What are you thinking?" she asked softly.

That I love you. He paused for a second, the answer ringing so clearly in his head, he wondered if he'd said it out loud.

"Zach?"

His mind and body raced in opposite directions, and it took him a minute to answer. "I—" He broke off as he looked up to find her staring at him, her features all dreamy and soft. A sleepy smile curved her lips in response to his own. But it was that same trace of vulnerability he'd detected last night that had him gathering her into his arms.

"I . . . what?" she prompted.

He wasted a second concocting a story, then gave up and told her the truth. "I was thinking about you."

She draped an arm across his chest and nestled her face into the crook of his arm. "What about me?"

Zach raked his fingers gently through her hair, lightly stroking her cheek and forehead, lingering on the outer shell of her ear, then resting on the soft curve of her shoulder.

What about me? Everything, he wanted to say. He had this sudden insatiable need to know everything about her, all the important things and all the stuff nobody else would care about. Nobody but someone who loved her. Nobody but him.

His arm tightened around her. "Tell me why you work so hard to grant wishes for these kids."

Dara managed to escape answering Zach's question until that afternoon behind the waterfall. They had hiked to the beautiful spot after a morning spent going over more of the technical aspects of the trip, followed by a lazy lunch during which another packet bit the dust. Dara smiled and leaned back against Zach's chest, letting the spray of the water raging down in front of them mist her skin, not caring that it soaked the front of her T-shirt.

"Should have brought the other two condoms with us." Even with his mouth pressed to her ear, he had to talk loudly to be heard over the pounding of the falls.

She tipped her head back and accepted his kiss, the motion as natural as if they'd been together like this for years rather than mere hours. She pushed that thought, and any others that could disturb this perfect day out of her mind. "It's just as well we didn't. I still need to hike back down the mountain tomorrow."

Zach's chuckle rumbled against her back. "Yeah, pacing is everything." He nuzzled her neck again. "Of course, there are other things we could do . . ."

Dara laughed, then choked on the sound as he rubbed his hips against her backside. "Zach, please." She wasn't at all sure what she was asking.

"I'll make you a deal."

She turned in his arms, wrapping hers around his waist. "You're going to barter with me for sex?"

"That depends."

"On what?"

"On whether the idea repulses you or turns you on."

She furrowed her brows and pretended to give it grave consideration. "I've already made it abundantly clear how much you repulse me." She squealed when he goosed her, then sighed dramatically. "Okay, so I'm turned on. What's your proposition?"

"I'll let you call the shots for the rest of the day if you'll answer one question."

"Oh, so magnanimous." He ran his hands over her hips and cupped her bottom. She shivered, and not because of her wet clothes. "Okay, okay. What's the question?"

His hands shifted to rest on her lower back, then he tilted her chin up. His expression grew more serious, and somehow she knew this was a side of Zach Brogan few people ever got to see.

"What do you want to know?"

"I want to know why you won't tell me about what

got you started with the Dream a Little Dream Foundation. Is it too personal, too painful?"

"That's two questions," she stalled, knowing it wasn't going to do any good this time.

"If you don't feel you can trust me with it—"

"No." She shook her head. "That's not it."

"Dara." He dipped his head and kissed her, the feel of his mouth on hers familiar and yet different. More gentle? Caring? No, it was something . . . deeper, something—

"I understand," he said roughly. He took her hand in his and started to lead her out from under the falls.

Ignoring the old protective instinct that had her automatically shying away from all thoughts of that part of her past, she tugged his hand, pulling him back around.

"His name was Daniel."

Zach froze. He had no idea what he'd been expecting, but hearing another man's name on her lips—and his reaction to hearing it said so reverently—was not it.

"Come on," he said, gently pulling her behind him, leading her along the small ledge that ran behind the waterfall.

"Zach!"

He kept on walking. "Watch your step," he said, keeping his mind on his feet. He realized that he was giving her time to evade the issue again. He wasn't too certain that hadn't been part of his sudden impetus to leave.

He didn't stop until they reached a partially shaded flat rock that jutted out over the calmer end of the pool.

He jumped onto it, then turned to help her up next to him. He sat facing the rocketing white stream of water and let out a breath he hadn't been aware of holding when she sat down in front of him. He spread his legs and pulled her back against his chest, looping his arms across her stomach.

"You can tell me this is none of my business," he said, giving her an easy out.

"When it wasn't your business, I didn't answer you."

Zach stilled for a second, then forced himself to relax. "So, what's changed?"

She tilted her head back to gaze up at him. "Before, you just wanted to know." She shifted, facing away from him again, but suddenly that wasn't enough. It wasn't right.

He pulled her around until she was facing him with her legs resting on either side of his hips.

"And now?" She tried to look away, but he captured her face in his hands. "Dara?"

She sighed, a faint but incredibly sweet blush stealing over her cheeks. He almost told her he loved her right then and there. Only her words stopped him.

"And now . . . I don't know." She pulled in a breath and held his gaze. "I guess it seems like now you need to know."

"Yeah," he said, softly. "I think I need to know everything about you."

He lowered his mouth to hers. He meant to stop at a short kiss, but it went crazy the minute her tongue touched his. Only when he felt her reach for the hem of his T-shirt did he find some semblance of sanity to stop her. "I want you, Dara," he said, his voice ragged against her hair. "But we need to talk about this first."

They both paused, then broke into pained laughter at the same time.

"Now I'm the sex fiend, and you want to talk," Dara said on a groan. "God help us both."

Zach grinned. "Honey, I'm beginning to think you're as beyond redemption as I am." He pulled her into a fierce hug. "But I wouldn't have it any other way."

He held her against him until their pulses slowed and their breathing was even. He didn't want to pressure her or badger her about this. It was enough that she was willing to tell him, he didn't have to hear it.

"You want to go back to camp? We can pack up and leave today. You've heard the whole spiel. This was the last place I needed to show you."

She didn't answer for a long time.

"I don't think I ever want to leave." She looked up, and ran the back of her fingers down his cheek, then a finger over his lips. "But I guess we have to."

"Yeah, we do. But—"

"But," she interrupted, "first I want to tell you about Daniel."

Zach nodded and tucked her head back on his chest, trying the best he could to make it easier on her, easier on himself.

"I met him when we were both freshmen in college."

"You went to George Mason, right?"

"Yes. Dane got a scholarship to UVA. It was the first time we'd been apart, really apart. After Dad died, and through the rest of high school, Dane helped me deal with it all. He understood how deeply I loved Dad. Mom blamed him for a long time for taking such a stupid risk. I guess Stan finally helped her deal with that. I sure wasn't much help. Not back then."

"What changed?"

She took a calming breath. "In high school and at college, I was always drawn to guys who were wilder. More like Dad, I guess."

"More like you," Zach interjected quietly.

Dara looked up at him, surprised. After a moment, she shrugged and laid her head back on his chest. "Maybe you're right. Dane said something like that to me too. I guess I didn't see it that way at the time."

"And Daniel was a wild man?"

"The wildest." She grinned up at him. "At that point anyway.

"He was a soccer player and a good one too," she went on, affection and pride in her voice. "Youngest team captain the league ever had. Determined to be a pro one day. His family didn't have much money, he was at school on a scholarship and he'd never really traveled. More than anything he wanted to see the world. And pro soccer was going to be his ticket."

She sighed. "It would have been too. But Daniel was young and strong and had that sense of immortality about him to such a strong degree that his judgment wasn't too sound. He tackled sports like a crazy man. He loved to have crowds cheering him on and chanting his name, but he also loved just about any other challenge. If he heard of a new sport, he had to try it. Nothing was out of bounds."

The dread Zach had been feeling began to creep in a cold, slithering band around his heart. Every word she spoke drew the band in tighter.

"We started talking about marriage when we were sophomores." She broke off for a moment, then after a deep breath, she said, "That spring he suffered a spinal cord injury while he was boogie boarding at Ocean City. He had to stay in a hospital near the shore for months. I took a leave from school to be with him. Eventually he was moved closer to home. Every minute I wasn't at school I spent by his bed. He never came out of his coma."

She snaked her arms around Zach's waist and hugged him tightly. "He died during my junior year." She swallowed hard. "He never got to see the world. Never got his wish," she whispered.

"And you didn't get yours either." She looked up, but Zach held her head to his heart and rocked her gently. "Shh. It's okay. I understand. I understand. You don't have to tell me any more."

"I was so angry at him. It was such a stupid waste. It wasn't until then that I understood what my mom had gone through."

"I'm sure she was a great help to you."

Dara shook her head against his shirt. "I couldn't tell her. Not then. She'd been through enough already."

"What about Dane?" Her brother had never said a word to him or Jarrett about any of this.

"He was so great after Dad died and when Mom remarried. If it wasn't for Dane, Mom and I probably wouldn't be speaking, and I know I'd never have learned to love Stan and appreciate him like I have. And he'd finally gotten free of all that, you know? He was off on his own for the first time, and when we'd talk on the phone, I'd never heard him sound so excited. Not ever. No way could I burden him with this."

Zach was stunned. "Surely he knew about it? I mean, when you left school—"

"I did tell him, eventually. But I made him promise not to tell anyone else. Mom and Stan had just retired and moved to their North Carolina dream home. I just couldn't do anything to ruin that. She deserved her happiness. So did Stan."

"But you did—"

"Yes," she broke in gently. "Eventually I did. And they were all great. I wouldn't have made it without their love and support."

She was trembling slightly and clutching him, and Zach wished like hell he'd never brought this up. Dear God it was no wonder she didn't want anything to do with him.

"I spent a lot of time at the hospital, and it was there that I heard about the Dream Foundation. To me Daniel was such a prime example of how important dreams are and how fleeting time can be. I volunteered for the group as a way to cope. After he died, I increased my time with them. It helped." She looked up, her eyes glimmering with tears, but her expression told him she'd found her peace. "You know?"

"Yeah," he said. "I know."

"After I got my business degree, I went to work for them full-time. I really felt like I was making a difference with the foundation. At first, it was for Daniel. But somewhere along the way that changed, and I was doing it for me."

"And for the kids."

"Yeah. It can be very frustrating and tedious getting the funding set up. But seeing those kids' faces. Well, it makes it all worth it."

He didn't think he could love her more than he did at that moment. Or feel so tortured knowing he'd never be able to tell her without hurting her.

Everything fell into place. Her feelings about the risks he took, why she'd so carefully shielded the part of herself that longed to be a bit wild. And though he knew in his heart that there was a world of difference between the carefully planned excursions that he conducted and the wild, careless antics of a college boy, he also knew how hopeless it would be to try and explain that difference to Dara.

He should be profoundly grateful she'd opened up and shared as much of herself with him as she had. And yet it was hard to feel that. He'd have to get past the huge yawning hole that was springing open inside him first.

He held her against him, rubbing her back and shoulders until the last of the tension seeped from her body. "Dara?"

"Hmm?"

"What did you think I'd do if you'd told me this the first time I asked? Back in your office that day?"

She stiffened, but only for a second. She raised her head and looked at him. "Honestly?"

"I don't think I want to hear this, but yes, honestly."

"I figured you'd tease me or make fun of it because of our past. Daniel will always be special to me, for a lot of reasons, and I guess I didn't want the Zach Brogan I remembered to touch that."

"Based on what you'd heard from Dane, I guess I can

understand why you thought of me as, how did you put it? Peter Pan with an American Gladiator complex."

Dara's smile was tentative. "I won't apologize for that. I didn't think you'd grown up or had a sense of responsibility."

"And now?"

Her smile faltered. "And now I'd like to think I can get past my feelings about what you do and judge you by the man you are."

He frowned. "I'm proud of what I do, Dara. In a way, albeit not nearly as altruistic as yours, I do the same thing as you. I fulfill dreams. Dreams of adventure and excitement. I give my clients the thrill of a lifetime."

"Not all people need to risk their lives to find adventure."

Zach resisted the urge to defend himself further. He knew what he was dealing with now. And as long as Dara still wanted to be with him, he had time to show her his side of the story. He kissed her soundly, then smiled down at her. "I think I can understand that. You've been one helluva an adventure for me."

She rolled her eyes. "Oh yeah, I'm a real walk on the wild side."

"Well, getting into a car with you isn't exactly for the faint of heart."

Dara stuck her tongue out at him.

"Hey, don't go waving that thing around unless you plan to use it."

She laughed and said, "I thought that was my line from after lunch."

He groaned and hugged her. Her return hug had him

truly relaxing for the first time since she'd begun her story. Hope began to fill that hole.

"Okay, okay. Change of topic." He set her back. "So," he said with a wide grin, "what do you think my chances are for getting this trip approved by the board?"

"I think they'll go for it." Dara kissed him, backing away before he could capture her head and take it deeper. "You did a great job."

"Better than you expected." It wasn't a question.

"Go ahead and gloat, I deserve a major I-told-you-so. But I still think this trip was necessary. You have to admit your background—"

Zach didn't want to get into that again and cut her off with another kiss, this one hotter and deeper. When she moaned and shifted against him, he lifted his head. "I want to have a barbecue for the kids and their parents after the board meeting."

Dara took a moment to focus on what he was saying.

"You're not a shoo-in, Brogan. But," she conceded, "should you get approval, I think a barbecue is a great idea."

"I thought it would give the kids and their parents a chance to meet the guys who'll run the trip. We can go over the details and answer any questions."

Dara framed his face with her hands and gave him a smacking kiss on the lips. "Have I told you I think you're wonderful?"

"Nope." But he sure as hell needed to hear it. He stood and pulled her up with him. "But I can think of a great way for you to show me."

"Zach, wha—? Oof."

Zach hoisted her gently over his shoulder, holding her with one arm across her thighs.

"What do you think you're doing?"

"Conserving your strength."

She didn't say anything for several seconds, and Zach braced himself for an unseen blow. Instead he felt her hands wiggle into the waistband of his shorts, and her wicked laugh filled the air.

"Keep it up and we won't make it back to camp," he warned.

"I'm trying to keep it up," she shot back. "And wasn't it you who said pacing was everything?"

"You'll pay for that one, Colbourne."

"I was counting on it, Brogan."

ELEVEN

Dara pulled her car into an empty space beside Zach's pickup. There were several other cars already parked in the huge yard next to Zach's rambling farmhouse. She scanned the wide open area in front, then headed around the side when she spied the picnic tables set up under the big oak trees in the backyard.

She spotted Zach almost immediately. Along with Beaudine and Scotty, he was standing by the grill, wearing a black T-shirt with "Badd Boyz Off Road Stuff" emblazoned in silver across the front and a ridiculously tall white chef's hat. She grinned.

They'd been back from the mountains for three weeks, and though she'd been very busy and he'd been gone for a good part of that time on another of his excursions, she didn't feel the least neglected. Far from it.

Her fears that the relationship would dissolve once they were off the mountain were never given the chance to materialize since Zach hadn't left her house until the following dawn. She'd been late for work for the first time in her life, and had still smiled throughout the entire morning staff meeting with Mr. Cavendish.

And before she had a chance to let worry or fear crawl inside of her, a pink gorilla had delivered a dozen balloons to her office late that afternoon after everyone else was gone. The attached note explained she was to drive to the address on the card if she was in the mood. She was in the mood.

Chinese carryout by lantern-light in the middle of the same field where they'd flown kites was his idea of a romantic candlelit dinner for two. She discovered it was hers also.

And even after he'd hopped a plane to the Yukon, she wasn't given any time to contemplate where this relationship might be headed or how foolish she was to continue it. He called from the airport to whisper hot, erotic things that were totally inappropriate for business hours, but she wouldn't have traded them for anything. And when he couldn't call, notes and other strange gifts arrived that alternately made her laugh, cry, or squirm uncomfortably in her seat wishing he were closer. Much, much closer.

Now, as she crossed the open yard, Dara fingered the small Inuit pouch hanging from her neck. It had come two days earlier with a note inside, written on paper cut in the shape of a moose head, telling her at which helipad to meet him. She'd gone to pick him up without a second's hesitation.

It had to end at some point. She wasn't so far gone that she'd deluded herself about that. Their lifestyles weren't long-term compatible. Even though he made a huge effort to be careful, she still worried about him the entire time he was away. And another painful realization had occurred to her when she sat at home wondering if he was okay and if he was doing something too crazy. Even if she could come to terms with his lifestyle, he might very well grow tired of hers. Or more to the point, of her, period. She might have reclaimed some of the wildness of her youth, but she knew she still wasn't the sort of woman to hold the attention of a man like Zach for any length of time. He needed someone who could climb mountains and ski down glaciers. She couldn't even handle a hot-air balloon ride. Besides which, no matter what she thought, and no matter how attentive he was being, he was hardly the type to consider a long-term arrangement of any sort, anyway.

Her steps slowed even though she never took her eyes off him; she even laughed as he expertly double flipped a burger and caught it on the spatula with a flourish.

Dara lifted the pouch and smiled wistfully, the slight pressure of her fingers crinkling the note still inside. Suddenly her hand tensed, pulling the leather thong taut. She felt his gaze on her like a physical touch and carefully schooled her expression to what she hoped was an open, friendly smile before lifting her head.

His grin still sent chills down her spine and did warm, funny things to the muscles of her inner thighs. God, she hoped this picnic didn't last too long.

Horrified that she'd even thought that, she lifted her face to the gentle breeze, hoping it would cool the hot flush she could feel in her cheeks as she crossed the remaining distance between them.

"Isn't it a bit early to be grilling the burgers?" she asked brightly. "The guests haven't arrived yet."

Zach shrugged and smiled. "I'm hungry."

"You're always hungry." Her gaze darted to Beaudine and Scotty. She had no idea how much they knew about her relationship with Zach, but she had a feeling she was about to find out.

"Insatiable." One word, dubious enough to be innocent, and she still blushed to the roots of her hair. He laughed. "Want one now? Or do you want to wait until later?"

"Later," she choked out, then turned resolutely to Beaudine. "It's nice to see you again." Dara's attention was instantly drawn to the front of the barbecue apron she wore. At first glance she thought it read: French Chef, but upon closer inspection, she saw the word "the" printed in small intricate script between the other two. She barely managed to swallow the laugh.

"Go ahead, *chère*. I don't wear it to make you frown."

"Has Frank seen that yet?" Zach asked, grinning.

Dara turned to him. "Frank's here?"

"Yeah." He nodded toward a huge shed near the rear fenceline that bordered a field. "He brought the rest of the buggies up so the kids could try them out. He's just running a last check on them."

"That's wonderful. I'm so glad you invited him." Suddenly Zach's question to Beaudine sank in and she turned back to the older woman, her gaze automatically dropping to the words emblazoned on her chest.

Before she could say anything, Beaudine leaned over and whispered in Dara's ear. "If it works, I let you borrow it." She laughed, and Beaudine joined her, though the expression in her eyes made it clear she knew exactly what was what between her and Zach. Dara didn't doubt it for a second.

"I'll let you know, okay?"

"Good enough." Beaudine grabbed the flipper from Zach's hand. "You go on and eat and take care of your guests as they arrive." She snatched the hat off his head and plopped it on her own. It caved in on one side, but the rakish angle somehow suited her perfectly. "Go on." She reached out to swat him, and only Zach's quick reflexes allowed him to walk away without wearing a greasy spatula print on his backside.

He snagged Dara's elbow and led her to the closest table. "Dane should be here shortly."

"Yeah," she answered, sitting down across from him. "He called this morning to ask if I wanted a ride."

Zach finished half the burger in two bites, swallowed, then said, "So why didn't you?" His grin told her he knew the answer, but wanted to hear her say it.

"I didn't want to wait for him. And I wasn't sure if you had plans for later . . ." She let the words drift off, but her smile was anything but shy.

"I'd have driven you home . . . whenever." He wiggled his eyebrows and quickly polished off the rest of the burger.

Just then gravel crunched along the drive behind them, and Dara turned to see two minivans pull up. "Looks like some of our guests have arrived."

Zach rose and dumped his plate in the trash can under a nearby tree. He took hold of her hand, and they walked across the grass to greet the kids that were noisily unloading from the vehicles. His hand felt big and strong and right, and Dara didn't give a thought to how the parents would react to seeing them together.

"Mr. and Mrs. Thomas, and Andie," she greeted the first group, "I'm Dara Colbourne and this is Zach Brogan."

"I'm so pleased to meet you finally," Mrs. Thomas said, shaking Dara's hand then Zach's. She glanced around. "This is some place you have here, Mr. Brogan. How many acres?"

"Please, call me Zach. This was my parents' home, I was raised here. It's about twenty acres total."

They were joined by the Johnsons and their son, Jonas. "Wow," Jonas piped up. "The grass must take forever to cut."

"Most of it is in those trees back there." He motioned past the field that spread out behind the fenceline. "But I have a tractor for the rest."

The youngster smiled, his chest puffing out a bit. "We have one too. The backyard is my job. Our tractor is probably smaller than yours." He looked momentarily glum about that, then grinned. "But so is our yard."

Dara was instantly captivated by the boy's open personality and easy charm. She glanced beyond him to find Andie had wheeled herself to the fringe of the small group. Dara introduced herself and Zach to Jonas's parents, then went over to Andie. "So, what do you think of all this?"

"It's okay," she said quietly, keeping her gaze averted.

Dara looked down at the ten-year-old's head, covered with barely a half inch of peach fuzz. She shot a questioning glance at her parents. They smiled reassuringly, but remained silent. Before Dara could continue talking with the girl, Zach stepped forward, bent down and whispered in Andie's ear.

Her face lit up like Las Vegas at midnight, and she tilted her head awkwardly up at Zach. "Really?"

"Really. Want to go check them out?"

"Yeah!"

Two more vans pulled into the lot, and Zach waved. He bent back down to Andie. "Mind if we take the rest of these guys with us?"

The girl's expression faltered for a moment. "You'll stay with me?"

Zach shot her his killer grin. "I've heard you're the hottest thing on wheels." He winked at her, and she giggled. "You couldn't pay me to stay away. I'd be honored."

She beamed. "Okay, we can wait."

Zach spoke to Andie's and Jonas's parents, but Dara didn't quite catch what he said. Then he strolled over to the newest arrivals. Introductions were made, and five minutes later Zach was leading all four kids toward the shed.

Dara grinned at the unusual parade of wheelchairs and crutches. Only Zach could make it all look perfectly natural.

"Like the proverbial Pied Piper," came a deep voice over her left shoulder.

She turned and smiled up at her twin brother. "Dane, you made it." She wasn't surprised to see a tie around his neck and fatigue lining his handsome face. She wasn't happy about it either, though she didn't say anything.

She'd needled him enough lately and knew when to back off. Her gaze was drawn back to Zach.

"Something in your eye?"

Confused, she looked back at Dane.

"No, my mistake." He smiled, the first she'd had from him in a while. "It's just that twinkle." He leaned in closer. "Wouldn't want to tell your brother anything, would you?"

Dara smiled, glad to hear the amusement in his voice. "No, nosy."

He laid his arm across her shoulder and turned them back toward the parents who had migrated toward the heavenly smells coming from Beaudine's grill.

"Are Jarrett and Rae coming?" she asked.

"I don't think so. I left messages at their house, but I don't think they're back yet."

Dara stole one last glance over her shoulder at Zach. He had an obviously smitten Andie in his arms and was leading the rest of the brigade into the shed. She smiled as she turned back to the parents, figuring she'd better hurry and explain about the buggies since they'd probably be making a grand entrance shortly.

Just as she was about to call their attention, Dane leaned down and whispered, "I'm glad to see you so happy, Dara. But tell me one thing?"

She looked up at him. "What?"

"Does he look at you the same way you look at him?"

She flushed. "I don't know. You'll have to watch him and find out for yourself," she shot back. "Can I ask you a favor?"

"Shoot."

"Let me know the results of your little survey?"

A flicker of concern surfaced in the normally unflappable calm of his hazel eyes. "Dara—"

She kissed him on the cheek. "Don't worry about it. It's fine, really," She grinned. "Really fine."

Dane stared at her for a couple of seconds, then nodded and droppd a kiss on her forehead before wandering off toward the grill.

Dara watched her brother's retreating form, then glanced back at the shed. Really fine. Yes, Zach was certainly that. She shouldn't have been surprised he was such a natural with the kids. But instead of underscoring her original opinion of him as a perennial Peter Pan, it made him even more of a man in her eyes. If she hadn't been sure she loved him already, the look of adoration in little Andie's eyes would have put her over the edge for sure. And she'd bet before the day was out, the rest of the kids would think he was a hero as well. She looked back at the parents. Something told her the adults would be won over just as easily.

She was rapidly coming to the realization that commitment or no, long-term or short, she was very likely not going to be the one to end this relationship. No matter how much wiser and less painful that might be.

"Zach, phone call," Scotty called out over the boisterous noise of the picnic, which was in full swing.

Zach shot him a questioning glance. Scotty nodded. "Keep the tension even, guys. And don't go too far. I'll be back shortly." He left Andie and the boys flying kites and headed for his office.

He picked up the phone and after one word and a

brief pause sent Scotty to find Dane. When he was alone, he said, "Jarrett, you're missing a great party."

Dara glanced up from the conversation she'd been having with Frank and two of the moms about doing some work on their electric wheelchairs. Frank had already announced he was donating the buggies to the kids.

Dara frowned. Zach was nowhere to be seen.

She politely excused herself and wandered off to find him, eventually going into the house, thinking maybe he was getting more supplies from the kitchen.

Voices echoed down the hallway. Male voices. One distinctly Zach's, the other equally recognizable as Dane's. She didn't take any real pains not to let them know she was coming, but about five feet from the door she heard Jarrett and Mr. Fujimora mentioned, although the rest was too mumbled to make out. Then she remembered Fujimora was the client Zach had been going to meet at Dulles that afternoon she'd first met with Frank.

She ducked her head around the doorway, not wanting to intrude, but never imagining she wouldn't be welcome. Her hello died on her lips.

Zach was pacing his office with the cellular phone to one ear, looking far more intense than she'd ever thought him capable of—except maybe when he was making love to her. And her brother behind Zach's desk, poring over a pile of maps.

"Tell him it's about three degrees north," Dane said, and Zach repeated the information into the phone. Her brother swore under his breath and shifted the ruler and compass he was using a bit, then swore again. "One degree west."

Dara shivered at Dane's tone. She knew the other guys at the National Transportation Safety Board called him "The Predator," but looking at him now she could believe he'd earned it.

Her gaze jerked up to Zach's pacing form, when he spoke. "Dammit, tell Fuji he'll just have to wait. No, I can't make it then. Tell him we'll meet at the arranged location on time." He stalked over to the desk and scanned the coordinates Dane was busy filling in. "It's not my fault he forgot to fuel the damn plane," he barked into the phone.

He was so wrapped up in his conversation, he hadn't seen her yet. *Who was this man?* she found herself thinking. And what was he talking about?

Was all this plotting and arguing about some trip he'd planned for this Fujimora character?

At her slight movement both Dane and Zach looked to the doorway. They didn't exactly seem happy to see her there. She contemplated going back out to the picnic and pretending she'd never seen any of this, but Zach's words stopped her.

"Okay, okay. I know. But I have to tell you, buddy, the timing really sucks." He kept his gaze on her while he spoke, and Dara could swear steam rose from her body. "Give me two days." He paused, then swore again. "And be prepared to do some explaining yourself when you and Rae get back." He listened for a second, then the first hint of a smile curved his lips. "Yes, that's exactly how it is. And I understand I have you to thank for that too. You just make damn sure I still feel like thanking you when this is over." A moment later he grunted, then handed the phone to Dane. "Finish it up while I go have a talk with your sister."

Dara wasn't sure she wanted to talk with him when he was like this, but he left her little choice.

"Come in here," he said, taking her arm and guiding her down the hall to a small den.

She cast a fleeting glance at her brother, certain he wouldn't approve of Zach's tactics any more than she did, but Dane was already deep in conversation on the phone and wasn't paying any attention to either of them.

As soon as Zach closed the door behind them, she pulled her arm from his and went to sit on the small couch. She crossed her arms in front of her, feeling suddenly cold and more than a little lost.

He sat down next to her, opened his mouth as if to speak, paused, then blew out a long breath.

Growing more bewildered by the second, Dara reached out and touched his arm. "Zach? What's wrong? Is it Jarrett? Or Rae? Did something happen to them on their honeymoon?"

He looked at her for a moment, then shook his head. "I'm sorry," he said quietly, his voice tired and fatigued, scaring her even more. "They're okay. But some . . . plans I'd made with him before he turned the company over have sort of changed at the last minute."

"You're scaring me, Zach. I've never seen you like this."

"Actually, I get like this whenever I'm in the middle

of planning a particularly difficult trip." He smiled. "Well, maybe not quite like this. Lately I spend more time planning trips than running them. It's as much of a challenge, sometimes the best part. It requires an incredible amount of patience and timing, knowledge and research. So many things could go wrong." He seemed to be talking more to himself.

"Is that what's happened? Did something go wrong on an excursion you planned for Mr. Fujimora? Was he a client of Jarrett's or something?" She thought he might have winced.

"Not exactly. This isn't what you'd call a normal sort of trip."

"Nothing you plan is normal."

"Thanks," he said dryly. "Well, there's no way to sugarcoat this and you're a big girl, so I'm just going to tell you straight out. I can't do the camping trip."

"What?" she asked, stunned and completely taken off guard. "What do you mean?"

"Now, don't go crazy on me. I'm not canceling it. I'll just be turning it over to Scotty. The rest of the crew will stay the same."

Dara's spine stiffened as the full implications of what he'd just said sank in. "Are you telling me that you're leaving these kids to take off to God knows where to help a client on some thrill-ride trip?"

"Jarrett's okayed the switch."

"Goody for Jarrett. What about those kids out there? You remember them, the ones who look at you like you're Superman or something. They've suffered enough disappointment, and if you think—"

"Dara," he lifted her hand and squeezed gently. "I'll explain it to them. They love Scotty, and the trip will go the same whether I'm there or not."

"So send Scotty out to play thrill-seeker with Mr. Fujimora."

"I can't do that this time."

She looked away, tugging her hand from his.

"If there was any other way." He pulled her back around. "Look at me. Do I seem happy about this?"

"No, but you're doing it anyway. Zach, I'm not going out there and ruining this picnic."

"Nothing's going to be ruined. And I'll handle it. Trust me."

"Yeah. Easy for you to say."

Tension and frustration entered his brown eyes. "Are we just talking about the camping trip here? I mean, is something else bugging you?"

"I thought I knew you, but now I'm beginning to think my first impression was more on the mark."

"Dammit, Dara. What I'm doing for Jarrett and Fuji is—" He broke off and swore under his breath.

"Is what, Zach? Make me understand."

"I can't tell you. Not yet at any rate. All I can say is that a while back I made a promise to Jarrett—"

"You made a promise to me and those kids too."

"Dara, I have obligations and responsibilities just like you, and they're just as important. I'm sorry for the change, but those kids will get the trip I planned for them. Just not with me. If I say I have to go, you can believe I have to. And if not, then maybe you really don't know me."

Dara's heart was pounding. "Maybe I don't." She yanked her gaze away from his. "Maybe I never really did."

He pulled her chin up to his, his eyes narrowed, his expression unreadable. "What are you trying to tell me? That because we have a difference of opinion about this trip, that's it? It's over? That's real mature, Dara."

"No," she shot back, anger filling the void where her heart used to be. "What's mature is fulfilling your obligations. What's mature is facing up to the fact that while we have great chemistry—"

"Chemistry? You mean because we're great in bed?"

Dara pulled away from him and stood. "That's what I mean. It's obvious we really don't have anything beyond that." If he'd gotten angry, she'd have been able to walk away. But he looked so wounded and hurt, her anger evaporated. She sighed and sank back down on the couch next to him. "You're right. It's silly to fight over this. You have your job to do, and I have mine. But you and I both knew this relationship was going to end at some point anyway."

"Speak for yourself," he mumbled.

Hope filled Dara's chest, but she squashed it. "I thought I could handle it, Zach. But face it, we really aren't compatible."

"Could've fooled me. I think we're damn good together." He turned to her. "And I'm *not* just talking about making love."

"Maybe we were," she whispered.

"Were, Dart?"

"Yeah," she said sadly. "You've shown me that it's

okay to risk a little, to live a little. I'll always be grateful to you for that."

"It's not your gratitude I want."

"The truth is, Zach, aside from my problems with your job, I'm not what you need either. Not really. You need someone who's more like you. Someone who can share and appreciate all of the aspects of who you are."

"And here I thought I was a grown man who could decide for himself what he needed." He stood and began to pace.

"Zach, please."

He turned on her. "Please what? Don't be sarcastic? Don't be angry? Well, excuse me. But, as you may or may not be able to tell, I'm not too thrilled about ending this relationship. So deal with it."

Dara's stomach hurt. This was harder than she thought, and she'd sworn she wasn't going to be the one to walk. But she knew she was right about this. And she realized now that prolonging it would only make it more devastating in the long run. Better just to finish it now and start wondering how the hell she was ever going to get over him.

"I still think I'm not the one for you." She raised her hand when he opened his mouth. "And while you're exciting and wild and the best time I've ever had, Zach—" Maybe she couldn't do this. Damn him for standing there all defiant and angry with those soul-searching brown eyes. "Zach," she whispered, looking away, "I just don't think I can be happy with a man who trots all over the globe, jumping off cliffs and out of planes, while I stay home."

"So come with me."

Her head shot up. "You know I can't. And that's not the answer anyway."

He heaved a sigh and sat down next to her, pulling her into his arms without warning. She knew she was in trouble when she made only a token protest.

She still didn't want to be anywhere else.

"Yeah, I know that," he said. "I guess I've known this was coming since you told me about Daniel." He held her for a long time, tucking her cheek against his heartbeat, smoothing her hair. "I hate this, Dara."

"I'm not real happy about it either."

"Then why the hell are we doing this to each other?"

"Because you are who you are. I don't want to change that. But I can't change my feelings either. I watched my mom fall apart when Dad died. And I was forced to sit by helplessly and watch as my own relationship ended tragically. And I find myself waiting for this one to fall apart too. I don't want to get to the point where you get bored with me because I'm not a thrill-seeker sort of woman, or I start resenting you for the risks you take. I don't want to spend every minute of the day and night worrying about what I'll do when you finally take one risk too many."

He lifted her face to his. "Is that what this is really all about? Losing another lover?" He shook his head. "Or is it your excuse?" She looked at him in shock. "You think I need another type of woman. But you're wrong, Dara. I've never even wanted a woman, not seriously, not like this, until you." He pressed his finger to her lips. "But I do understand that I'm not what you need. I wish like hell that weren't true, but if I'd make you crazy or miserable, it doesn't matter why. Maybe this is for the best."

He took a deep breath, then let it out slowly. "Hard as that is to accept." He tugged her closer to his chest, then tucked his hand under her hair and tilted her head back. "But I'll be damned if I can let you go without one last kiss."

TWELVE

Dara didn't have time to decide whether it was a good idea or not. His mouth was on hers, hot, hard, and needy, and she simply responded.

His hands moved up and down her back, wove into her hair, traced her ears, cupped her cheeks. His mouth moved over hers possessively, taking not asking, giving without waiting to be invited.

Dara's head swam, her heart pounded, her skin heated, but before she could muster any sort of control, it was over.

Zach lifted his head and carefully sat her away from him, his hands heartbreakingly gentle. His gaze never left hers, even as he stood. "I have to go out and talk to the group about this. Then Dane and I have to leave. He's helping me with some of the transportation. Beaudine and Scotty can handle the rest of today, so if you want to—"

"I'm not leaving. Even though the barbecue was your idea, these kids are my responsibility."

A sad smile curved his beautiful mouth. "I hope they know how lucky they are to have someone like you in their corner." He walked to the door, turned the knob, then paused. His head dropped forward until his forehead rested on the frame. He stood like that for so long, Dara was halfway to her feet when he finally turned back to her. The leashed power of his gaze made her sit back down.

"I know I shouldn't say this. Especially not now. But you are my ultimate thrill, Dara Colbourne. Nothing and no one has ever compared. And if I travel for the next hundred years, I don't think I'll ever be as happy as I have been these last few weeks." His smile faded, and his voice grew rougher. "And damn if I don't love you like hell on fire."

Dara couldn't move, couldn't breathe. "Zach—"

Just then someone pounded on the door. "Brogan? You about done? Let's get a move on." It was Dane.

He never took his eyes off her. "Yeah, be right there. Do me a favor, Dart?"

"What? Yes." *Anything*, she felt like saying, but couldn't. Her mind was still replaying his last words, trying to comprehend that he'd really said them.

"Find someone who makes you happy. Make your dreams come true. No one else can, you know. You deserve it. Just don't forget me." He winked and ducked out the door.

Dara slumped back on the couch, feeling emptier and more alone than she'd ever felt in her life.

Forget him? Never.

She forced herself to ask the question: How long would it take him to forget her? The answer should have given her the comfort she needed, the conviction that she'd done the right thing. For both their sakes.

It didn't even come close.

Dara rested her elbows on her desk and flipped open the second folder on her stack. Arandon, Inc. wanted to fund a wish currently on her list. She smiled, but after opening the next file, the smile faded. Another one. That brought the total to six donations made specifically for wishes on her list in the last three weeks. Three weeks. It had been four weeks since she'd seen Zach.

Four miserable, lonely weeks. No letters. No calls. No funny gifts. No Zach.

The only thing she knew was that the camping trip had been a smashing success, and if the cards and notes she'd received from the kids and their parents were any indication, the kite-flying party Zach had treated the kids to a week later—his version of an apology—had been an even wilder success. She didn't doubt it. Zach was the sort of person that brightened the lives of everyone he knew. No matter how briefly.

Of course when that bright light was gone, it was amazing how incredibly dark a place could be.

Don't forget me. Impossible. Not if she lived to be a thousand.

She rested her forehead in her hand, fighting the tightness in her throat as images of Zach laughing, Zach winking, Zach dancing, and Zach making love to her all raced through her brain like a fever.

She blinked hard several times and purposely shifted her attention to the folders. And now it was becoming increasingly hard to ignore that he was continuing to affect people's lives—hers included—by getting his clients to donate funds to Dream A Little Dream. She knew without a doubt there had been no coercion, the donations made willingly.

Her resistance weakened, and she gave voice to the thought that had plagued most of her waking moments and all of her sleeping ones. "I want Zach Brogan back. I may be a masochistic idiot for loving a crazy man again, but I'm an even bigger idiot for making him go away."

The bigger question was, did he still want her?

A hard rap on her door brought her head up. Her mouth dropped open in surprise when Jarrett McCullough strolled into her office.

"Jarrett? What are you doing here?"

He was the sort of man who exuded athletic grace but in a dark, quiet sort of way. His hair was blacker than midnight, and he had gray eyes that could make a woman shiver. Hard and always in control. That was Jarrett. At least that was the Jarrett she used to know.

He was still all those things, but . . . Maybe it was his eyes, Dara thought. She wouldn't say they were softer, but they were definitely more open.

"Nice to see you again too," he said sardonically as he took a seat across from her.

"I'm sorry," she said smiling, then froze when a sudden shiver of apprehension crawled down her spine. "Is something wrong? Did something happen?"

"No. At least no one's sick or injured or anything, if that's what you mean." He sat down and leaned back, more relaxed than she remembered him ever being before.

"Is Rae here with you? I'd love to meet her. I'm really sorry I couldn't make the wedding."

"No, she's not, but she'd like to meet you too. And we missed you, but Dane said you were on a trip with some foundation kids. We both understood."

He was being perfectly sociable, but Dara couldn't shake the feeling that something else had brought him here. "I love seeing you again," she said. "But I get the feeling this isn't a social call."

"Not in the normal sense."

This time her smile came easily, if a bit sadly. "I've become real familiar with the abnormal lately."

"Actually, that's sort of why I'm here. I promised Zach a month ago I'd do this."

"Zach? He sent you here?" Now she was confused.

"Not directly. Actually, he let me off the hook right after he got back from Tibet."

"Tibet?"

Jarrett's eyes narrowed. "You still don't know what he was doing, do you?" He swore under his breath. "I knew I should have come sooner. Rae told me—" He cut himself off with a chopping hand motion, then looked up at her.

Dara lifted her hand to stop him. "It doesn't make a difference."

"It damn well should," he said sharply. "I can't believe you were so hardheaded and unfair."

"Hardheaded and unfair!" she shot back before she could stop herself. His attack was unexpected, but her anger died quickly. Now she slumped back in her seat. "The reason I said it didn't matter, is because I realize now that if he said it was important, it was. I don't have to know why."

"He got one of my operatives out of a very sticky situation. It was something I had set up before I married Rae. Things went real wrong, real fast, and Zach got in there and got the job done when no one else could have."

Dara was stunned. "Has he done this for you often?"

"Not often. But when it counts he is always there. He's the one that got Rae out of Bhajul for me. He's saved my butt many a time. I'm here because I feel responsible for what's happened between you two. I wanted you to understand just what you've given up."

"I know just what I've given up, Jarrett," she said quietly, more than a little moved by such a strong declaration of allegiance coming from a man as closemouthed and taciturn as Jarrett. "First, thank you for the generous donation you made to the foundation. Those kids had a blast."

"You do good work here, Dara. I'm just glad I could contribute. But about Zach—"

She cut him off again. "It's not about the trip, Jarrett. I didn't know the important work he was doing for you, but it goes further than that. Deeper than that."

"Is this about Daniel?"

Now he'd really shocked her. "How did you know about that?"

He shrugged. "Dane needs an outlet too every once in a while. He was worried about you back then. You took on a pretty rough deal. It never went past me. I just listened."

She nodded. "Zach's job is part of it, Jarrett. I lost my dad and Daniel because they took foolish risks. I didn't think I could handle wondering every time Zach walked out the door if it would be the last time I'd see him. And I knew I couldn't bear to see someone with his vibrancy lying lifeless and vacant in a hospital bed."

"You said 'didn't'—does that mean you've had a change of heart?"

A small smile curved her lips. Jarrett didn't miss anything. "My heart has been his since about a minute after he walked into my office. And no, I haven't changed my mind about worrying about him. I don't think that's something that will ever go away. So, if I've already signed on for the worst part of it, then I want the best part too."

"Then what the hell's the problem?" Jarrett asked with his customary bluntness. "If you love him, why are you sitting around here hating life while he's doing the same thing halfway around the globe?"

Dara looked up. "He's hating life?"

"What in the hell did you think he was doing? The man tells you he loves you, and you dump him."

"He told you he said that?"

"He didn't have to, Dara. But if I was in any doubt, Beaudine set me straight when she tracked me down two days ago." His mouth lifted into a small smile. Dara couldn't recall ever seeing him do that before.

"Rae must be one hell of a woman," she whispered, in awe.

The smile deepened. "You'd better believe it."

Dara recalled what he'd said. "Beaudine called you?"

"Apparently she had reached a, uh, rather delicate moment in her . . . negotiations with Frank, when

Zach rudely interrupted. Rae was convinced I needed to do this in person. So here I am."

"Oh no, you came back early from your honeymoon just—"

Jarrett lifted his hand. "Rae was right. And don't worry, I intend to get back to our honeymoon just as soon as I'm done here. Even Beaudine won't be able to track us down." He leaned forward. "But this time I'm glad she did. Seems Zach's been a bit over the edge lately, even for him. Taking on more trips and maybe a few too many risks."

A sick knot twisted inside her stomach. "He's not, I mean, I know he risks his life all the time, but he's not—" She took a breath but couldn't seem to find enough available air. "He wouldn't intentionally, you know—"

"No," Jarrett said immediately. "Not Zach. He's scrupulous about margin of risk and safety and all that. He wouldn't be so successful if he wasn't. But Beaudine demanded I talk some sense into him, immediately. I didn't refuse."

A small smile threatened despite her moment of panic and the still overwhelming confusion. "I don't blame you. I hear she was a pretty hot contender on the gator wrassling circuit."

Jarrett sobered a bit and added, "Even Frank was concerned."

"Frank?"

"Did Zach ever tell you how he met Frank?"

"No," she said, wondering briefly about all the other things she'd never learned about him, things she had a deep hunger to know. "No, he never did."

"Frank has always been a mechanic, but he used to

work on planes. He was one of the best. Zach used him almost exclusively with his planes."

"He has planes?" She raised her hand, thinking of mountains and hot-air balloons. "Never mind. Dumb question. Go on."

"Frank was working for Zach when there was a freak accident in the hangar. It's complicated, but basically, a part of the plane fell off and landed on Frank's back. Cracked a couple of vertebrae. Even though it was ruled an accident and no one, including Frank, blamed Zach, Zach still took it really hard.

"Frank's insurance didn't go real far, and Zach helped him out. He was sort of the motivating force behind getting Frank back into a viable career. He was the one who financed the garage. I think he's still a partner."

Dara's throat tightened. And she'd accused him of not paying the man. "I'm not surprised."

Jarrett studied her for a while, then said, "Is there another reason you called it off?"

She looked steadily at the man who was responsible for her finding Zach again in the first place. It took her a moment to gather her courage, then put into words for the first time the truth Zach had known that day in his den. "Me. Me being afraid to go after what I want. He goes to some pretty far extremes to satisfy his desires. I'm not like that, and it was easy to tell myself I couldn't compete. No risk there, right?"

"Did he ever ask you to compete? He loves you, Dara. I know he's never felt like this about anyone before. Maybe you have to trust that. Trust him to know what he wants."

"The one I have to trust is myself." She sighed. "I think I've dealt for so long with how unfair life is, that somewhere along the way I decided it was easier to make excuses than to take chances. That way I had more control."

"Well then if you—"

"Where is he now?" Dara interrupted. "I suddenly realized I'm having this conversation with the wrong person." She grinned, and her heart began to pound. "Nothing personal."

Jarrett didn't even blink. "Skiing. In Hawaii."

"Hawaii? Skiing? It's the end of July."

"Yeah, they had some freak cold front that prolonged the season. Once in a lifetime kind of conditions. Helicopter in and ski the volcanoes or something. Zach had a couple of guys pay him double to take them."

Dara flipped her folders shut. For Zach skiing in Hawaii made perfect sense. "Well, the wishes on my list are being granted at a pretty alarming rate, so I'm sure even Cavendish will agree that I can take a short leave."

Jarrett smiled and stood.

Dara scooted out from her desk and stopped in front of him, then impulsively reached up and hugged him. He stilled for a moment, then hugged her back. "Thank you, Jarrett."

"I didn't do anything." She shook her head and started to argue, but he cut her off. "Just invite us to the ceremony."

She grinned and nodded. "You know, the last time I saw Zach, he told me the only person who could make my dreams come true was me. He was right." She bussed Jarrett on the cheek and grabbed her purse. "He also told me to find the right man and marry him. That's just what I intend to do."

Dara was halfway down the hall to Cavendish's office when Jarrett called out, "Give 'em hell, D'Artagnan!"

Skiing in Hawaii sucked. Zach leaned on his poles and looked down over the rim. Bradley and Schuster had just schussed over the edge and were hammering down the perfect pristine slope. He couldn't work up even a shred of their enthusiasm. He didn't feel like skiing.

Just like he hadn't felt like diving off the coast of Peru or riding the rapids in Colorado.

"The hell with this," he said. He was no good to his clients, his employees, and most of all not himself. He stamped his poles deeper into the snow. He wanted Dara.

And as soon as this trip was over, he vowed silently, he was heading back home to get her. He'd camp on her doorstep, kidnap her, take her away to the mountain, something, anything. Whatever it took to make her understand her worth—to him, to herself. But what he wasn't going to do was leave her. Not ever.

The distant whup-whup sound of a helicopter penetrated his thoughts. He shaded his eyes with his hand and scanned the sky, locating the small private craft. It was heading right for him.

Several minutes later it had landed on the plateau about two hundred yards to his left. The hatch opened, and Zach knew then Beaudine was right. He had gone over the edge. Otherwise he'd have to believe that a pink gorilla had just climbed out of that chopper.

It got harder to justify the hallucination as it walked toward him. The beast poked one furry paw at the label on the package which said "Zach Brogan," then pointed at Zach.

Zach nodded dumbly. "I'm Brogan."

The monkey handed him the small loosely wrapped bundle with a bright red bow on top. Not knowing what else to do, Zach took it. The big neon ape simply bowed and headed back to the chopper.

"Thank you," Zach called out belatedly. Only when the helicopter was a dot in the sky did Zach look back at the package in his hands. "What the hell." He pulled off his gloves and opened it. A small carved dragon fell out. A smile started to curve his lips as his mind raced to come up with a list of reasons not to get his hopes up.

There was a small scroll tucked in the loop of the tail. He pulled it out and uncurled it. "If you're in the mood," he read out loud, "meet me on the beach in front of the Kontiki at midnight. I promise not to breathe fire . . . unless you want me to."

There was no signature. But Zach's pulse was already pounding and his adrenaline was pumping before he'd gotten halfway through it.

"No," he told himself. "She'd never come all the way out here." She'd have to fly for one thing. A very long flight. But even as he tried to tamp down the overwhelming rush, he was tucking the dragon and the bow into a zippered pocket.

He poled back to the edge, and scanned the perfect twin snakelike tracks cut into the slope below him, then stopped and pulled off his glove again. He yanked the note out and reread it. Twice.

He was in the mood all right. And if he had anything to do with it—and he planned to—he expected to be in the mood for the rest of his life.

With an avalanche-threatening rebel yell, he shoved off over the edge and shot straight down the mountain.

Zach found her in a private cove, standing ankle-deep in the midnight surf. A stunningly erotic sarong wrapped around her lithe body, a beautiful hibiscus blossom tucked into her shoulder-length brown hair. She couldn't have possibly heard his bare feet on the sand, but she turned and looked straight at him when he was still twenty yards away.

He stopped and stared at her, unable to believe she was truly there. "You look like a pagan goddess," he said. "My own Venus."

Her gaze ran over him slowly, making his pulse race and his body harden. She walked toward him. His senses screamed, his muscles tightened, his mind focused with intense precision and total clarity on her. Only her.

He'd never, in his whole life, experienced a rush like this. He thought he might spontaneously combust if she came any closer; he thought he might go insane if she didn't. And he knew he'd die if she ever left him again.

She stopped a foot away and looked up into his eyes. For all her outward boldness and confidence, the trace of vulnerability was still there. It undid him completely, and he reached for her, pulling her hard against him, wrapping her as tightly into his arms as he could.

"Are you really here," he whispered into her hair, "or have I just conjured you up from desperation?"

"I'm really here," she said softly.

His heart ached, and his eyes burned. "Don't ever leave me again," he said roughly.

"No. Never again."

He pulled her head back and lowered his mouth to hers, wanting to keep his kiss gentle and thorough, but at the first taste he lost it. He took her mouth, begged her with his lips, his tongue, his moans, his every breath to take him also.

"You *are* like fire," he murmured against her throat. He trailed kisses along her neck, drew his tongue over her pulse, nipped at her ear. "I won't ever get enough of you. Believe that. We can work the rest out."

Dara turned her head and nuzzled the crook of his neck, then tilted her head back and looked up into his eyes. All flickers of uncertainty were gone. Zach grinned broadly, his heart so full, he thought it would burst.

"I think I already have," she said. "At least for me. I trust you to know what you want, to believe in your love. You were born to be wild, and I wouldn't have you any other way. But I have to have you." Her smile broadened. "And you know I'm serious if I flew in a plane for what seemed like six lifetimes to get to you."

"You didn't have to do that," he said, his tone hushed and fierce. "One call and I'd have been there."

"I couldn't wait. I just shut my eyes and focused on you the whole time." She tipped up on her toes and pressed a soft kiss to his lips. Then, framing his face with her hands, she focused everything she had on his gaze. "But most importantly, I trust in myself. If it's possible to be what you need, then I'll be it. Because more than anything else, Zach Brogan, I love you like hell on fire."

His breath caught. "I didn't think I was ever going to hear you say that." Her smile was lost under the pressure of his mouth on hers. "I love you," he said against her mouth, then again against her cheek, all along her neck and whispered into her ear.

He ran his hands all over her, his lips following. She moaned and moved against him. Their hips quickly found a rhythm until Zach pulled away, breathing heavily.

"If I don't get you somewhere a bit more private," he ground out, "we're going to make love right here on the beach."

She laughed and rotated her hips against him again. "And here I thought you were the thrill-seeker in this relationship."

Zach growled and caught her hips in his hands, holding her tight to him. "I'll thrill you."

"You already do," she gasped. "And I've become addicted to it. To you."

"If you let me, I'll thrill you for a lifetime."

She stilled. "Is that a proposal?"

He pulled her head to his. "That's a promise." His kiss was a physical avowal of his words.

When he let her up for air, she said, "Starting now?"

"Right now."

Dara stepped away, and with a very wicked smile she tugged at the one and only knot holding up her sarong.

Zach choked on a laugh. "You keep doing stuff like that and we may not live long, but we'll go out in a blaze of glory." He reached for the waistband of his white beach pants, then groaned when she started to sway her hips. "Oh God, you're going to kill me even before the honeymoon."

She moved in a circle, beckoning him with graceful movements of her hands. "You took hula lessons?" he managed to ask, his voice hoarse.

She smiled and continued her seductive invitation. "It's not cliff diving," she said, "but it's a start."

Zach stepped out of his pants and yanked off his floral print shirt. He grinned when her fluid motions jerked to a halt with a sudden shiver. "Somehow I don't think I'll be diving off as many cliffs in the future," he said, and stepped closer. "In fact, I doubt I'll be leaving home much at all."

"And here I was all ready to ask you to take me hot-air ballooning."

"I love you just the way you are, Dara." She moved closer to him, and he could barely breathe. "Don't ever do anything you don't really want to." His voice was more a raspy whisper.

She put her hands on his chest and let them slide downward. "Oh, I want to," she said, her voice dark and husky. She looked up at him. "Thrill me, Zach."

And he did.

EPILOGUE

They were married one month later in the middle of their field under the bright summer sunshine.

The bride arrived by motorcycle and wore an all-white off-the-shoulder formfitting gown. A very short gown. The groom wore black tie and tails and a huge grin.

The maid of honor wore hot-pink.

The best men wore white tails with matching hot-pink ties and cummerbunds. The one in the wheelchair only had eyes for the maid of honor.

The traditional wedding march boomed from the speakers, and Zach turned to watch his bride walk down the flower-strewn, makeshift aisle.

The last notes faded as Dara joined Dane under the white linen awning. Dane handed his sister over to his best friend, shook his hand, then turned to the minister. "I give this woman." His strong face was full of pride as he answered the minister's next question. "I'm her brother."

Shoulders squared, his love evident to all, Dane bent and gave her a brief hug, then stepped back to join the small throng of friends and family.

Dara took a deep breath and peered through her veil at the most handsome man in the world. The man who in a few short minutes would be her husband. Her knees trembled, her body tightened in anticipation.

"You're so damn beautiful," Zach said in an awe-struck whisper.

"So are you," she whispered back, her eyes shining.

"I love you," they said at the same time, then reluctantly dragged their gazes away from each other to answer the minister's questions and repeat their vows.

A short time later, the minister said, "I now pronounce you man and wife."

Amid raucous cheering Zach lifted her veil. He grinned and leaned down. "Hi, wife," he said softly.

"Hi, husband."

Her smile was sweet and shy and sexy, and in front of God and everybody he kissed his new wife with all of the love and passion she so easily inspired in him, bending her back over his arm in his fervor.

The crowd wholeheartedly approved, as Shocking Blue's rendition of "I'm Your Venus" boomed out of the speakers.

When he pulled her up to an unsteady stand, she held on to her headpiece and smiled up at him. "I love you."

"Yeah, it's incredible, isn't it?"

"It's perfect." She breathed deeply, wanting this moment to last forever. But impatient for all the moments to come, she faced the group. "Ready?" she called out.

Everyone crowded forward as she turned her back.

"One, two, three!"

The bouquet landed on Frank's thighs. His hand darted out quicker than a snake, and an instant later his lap was occupied by a spluttering Beaudine. Amid whoops and much cheering, Frank laid one on her. When he lifted his head, a dazed Beaudine was clutching the bouquet.

And they dined on red velvet wedding cake, toasted each other with Dom Pérignon, danced to Mozart and the Moody Blues, and flew kites by the light of the moon.

Dear Reader,

Well, now you've met my second musketeer, Zach Brogan. I hope you had as much fun watching him take the big fall as I did sending him on the plunge. I hope you've also met my first musketeer, Jarrett McCullough, in **SURRENDER THE DARK.**

But now it's time for the last musketeer to meet his destiny. Dane Colbourne has been there for his two friends and his twin sister through thick and thin. In **MIDNIGHT HEAT,** it will be their turn to come to the rescue.

Dane is my intense, focused hero. In his job as an investigator for the National Transportation Safety Board, his ability to hunt down every detail and solve the sometimes impossible mysteries of major airline disasters has earned him the nickname "The Predator."

His latest hunt puts him hot on the trail of one of the best air traffic controllers in the industry. Is she guilty of negligence? Did she almost cause the deaths of over one hundred people? Or is her improbable story of a third plane true?

The facts prove she's guilty. And Dane is a man who has built his whole life on tangible proof. But her eyes, her voice, everything about her, makes him want to believe she's telling the truth. Damaging evidence continues to pile up as their personal relationship begins to spiral out of control. Will Dane be able to vindicate her? Time is short, the pressure is on, and if he fails, not only will he lose the one woman who has found the way to his heart, but he may lose his own soul as well.

For the first time in his life, Dane is forced to ask for help. It's all for one and one for all in the exciting conclusion of The Three Musketeers trilogy.

Look for **MIDNIGHT HEAT** to burn a path to your store next month. Happy swashbuckling!

Donna Kauffman

The Three Musketeers: MIDNIGHT HEAT
by Donna Kauffman

The Predator was coming. For her.

Adria Burke had heard the whispers over an hour ago as she sat in the small airless office deep in the bowels of Washington D.C.'s Metropolitan Airport.

The Predator. The National Transportation Safety Board investigator Dane Colbourne. The man who never left a case unsolved. The man now assigned to cover "the incident."

Her incident.

Adria watched the hour hand click onto the four. Four *a.m.* She huffed out a sigh and shifted her gaze to the coffee dregs at the bottom of her cup. Other than a lengthy and at times heated discussion with her supervisor, Mark Beck, she hadn't spoken to a soul since midnight.

"Where is this guy?"

It was at least the hundredth time she'd wondered it, but the first time she'd said it out loud. The sound of her own voice, tired and scratchy, did little to boost her morale.

She'd reviewed in exacting detail her role in the midair collision that had taken place shortly after she'd assumed her position in the control tower. And each time she'd come to the same conclusion: It wasn't her fault. If she were faced with the same horrifying scenario again, she'd make the same decisions, issue the same commands. That the two pilots, their crews, and passengers had somehow come out of it safely had been a miracle.

But that a major disaster had been averted was not the issue. Two planes had collided, and now she was under investigation. If Dane Colbourne reached the conclusion that she was negligent, she'd likely pay the price of being forced to leave.

Adria had considered her assignment to Metro a huge personal and professional victory. Losing it, after she'd fought so hard, after the private hell she'd been through . . .

It was simply unthinkable.

But lose it she very well might. And then she could kiss her career goodbye. Unless she could get someone to believe in *her* side of the story. Beck hadn't wanted to hear about the fact that up until seconds before the Liberty and AirWest planes collided, there had been a third plane—a primary target—on her display, in the same areas as the other two planes. A plane whose direction and speed had decided her on her course of action.

Where in the hell had that damn plane come from? And more important, where had it gone? It had simply disappeared from her display. And why wouldn't anyone believe her?

That the last man she had a shot at convincing was referred to in awed whispers as The Predator only increased the dull throbbing in her temples.

She looked to the door, willing it to open. Willing the man she was waiting for to enter.

She treated her tired mind to the pleasure of imagining what Colbourne must look like. Over fifty, beady eyes, thinning hair held in place with BrylCreem. Short, stocky, serious attitude problem. Anal retentive as hell. He was probably ex-military, the sort who ate gravel for breakfast, then spat it at everyone who got in his path the rest of the day.

Jack Nicholson's face swam into her mind. "Ooooh, The Predator," she whispered in mock horror.

That very instant the door swung open.

Choking hard on the laugh that had crept up into her throat, Adria stared in shock at the man who entered the room.

So much for over fifty. He couldn't be much older than her own thirty-one. Short was definitely out as well; he was easily six feet, with well-distributed muscles. She didn't catch his eyes as he passed, so beady was still a possibility. What she did see of his face was all strong, clean angles. Now she understood what chiseled features meant. His hair wasn't oily or thinning. It was thick, wavy, and light brown, cut razor sharp in a way that enhanced the chiseled look.

But it wasn't any of those things that took her aback completely.

It was the crisp, white, perfectly tailored tuxedo with tails he was wearing.

Any hope she'd had of regaining her composure fled when he stopped at a metal desk and turned around. His cummerbund was a painfully bright fuchsia. She had no idea where he'd found a rose to match. But there was one, pinned to his white satin lapel.

This was The Predator?

Adria barely restrained herself from asking how Barbie had ever let him leave the dream house.

He slapped a stack of folders onto the desk. The chair squeaked as he pulled it out, and protested even louder when he sat. He said nothing, simply began to scan the contents of the top file. He had yet to look in her direction.

Irritation crowded out Adria's surprise. Well, she hadn't been completely skunked. She'd apparently hit the bull's-eye on his severe attitude problem. And from the arrow-straight back and perfectly squared shoulders to the neatly piled folders, she bet she wasn't too far off on the anal retentive assessment either. Even his rose hadn't wilted.

Although he probably wouldn't appreciate her concern, she took a second and tried to dredge up some sympathy for him. He'd obviously been dragged away from some important function. She half wondered if it wasn't his own wedding. That wouldn't surprise her in the least.

A full minute passed and still no sign that he was aware of her. She sighed in disgust. If he'd thought to ambush her with his get-up and intimidate her with his silent treatment, then he was in for a rude surprise. She'd learned that game at the feet of a master.

She stood and held out her hand. "Mr. Colbourne, I presume?"

No response came while he continued his silent study. Adria felt the heat of anger climb into her cheeks. Unwise words were on the very tip of her tongue when he finally spoke.

"Sorry to keep you waiting," he said, not looking up, nor sounding the least bit sorry. In fact, there was no emotion in his voice at all.

She was sorely tempted to ask him if he always conducted his interrogations in formal wear, just to see if she could get a reaction—any reaction—out of him. The impulse was instantly forgotten when he suddenly raised his head and looked directly at her for the first time.

"You can take a seat, Ms. Burke. This will probably take a while."

Adria's still proffered hand dropped to her side while she stared at his eyes. Hazel. A muted green with just a hint of gold. Faintly bloodshot, with little fatigue lines at the corners. All in all, not the kind of eyes that should warrant any special attention.

So why did they capture hers?

A shiver tickled her spine. She had the odd sensation

that he was testing her. She felt . . . well, the only word she could think of was pinned. And she really hated it.

He dipped his chin, his gaze flicking to the chair behind her. "I'm ready to begin."

The reality of the situation hit her. He was calling the shots. He was also her last hope. She'd learned the value of asserting herself, but she hadn't forgotten that timing was everything. And now wasn't the time. So she merely nodded, then sat down.

"I'd like to ask you some specific questions about your actions immediately after taking control of your position."

She swallowed hard against the almost desperate need to blurt out her view of the night's events, forcing him to listen and believe. She'd tried that with Beck and had gotten nowhere. Instead, she curled her fingers into fists, then slowly, purposefully relaxed them. A stress management technique she'd mastered during her divorce. Or precisely, *en*during. Studiously avoiding The Predator's attire, she focused on a point between his eyes and blanked her own expression to match his.

"Ask away," she said, proud of the steady tone.

"I understand that shortly after taking control of your position last night, you issued an altitude change to Liberty flight 576. Is that correct?"

"Yes, it's correct." She didn't mention the fact that Pete Moore, the controller who held the shift before her, had left the plane dangerously close to the AirWest plane. "There was a third plane—" she continued on.

"Please, Ms. Burke," he interrupted. "Just answer my questions yes or no for the time being."

Of all the . . . Stay cool. Stay calm. One benefit of being an air traffic controller was the conditioned response to high-stress situations. This certainly qualified.

Adding control freak to her mental description list of The Predator, she clenched her teeth and said, "Yes, sir."

He held her gaze for an interminable second, then dropped it back to the notes. "The Liberty pilot reports you then issued a radar warning about a primary target, followed by new coordinates and another change in altitude."

"Yes."

"You then issued new coordinates to the AirWest pilot, after which the pilot received a TCAS warning," he said, referring to the Traffic Collision Avoidance System, a mechanism on board each aircraft. "You countermanded that warning due to the supposed involvement of the primary target."

She remained silent.

After a long while, he gave her a hard look. "Ms. Burke?"

"Yes?" Adria blamed exhaustion for her irrational need to bring him down a notch. But really, the situation was tense enough without his attitude filling up the room.

"You have no response?"

"Yes, I do. But you didn't ask me a direct yes or no question. I was simply trying to follow orders. Sir."

A scowl began to form in his mouth. Adria couldn't suppress the pleasure she took in that tiny victory. So, he could feel an emotion after all. Even if it was irritation.

The Predator tossed his pencil on the desk and leaned back in his chair. "It's been a long night, Ms. Burke. I really don't have the patience to sit here and play games with you."

Adria imagined he had unlimited patience. Most hunters did.

"My goal here," he continued, "is determining the cause of the incident. I have an AirWest pilot who says he responded to your directions after the TCAS, only to scrape wing tips with the Liberty, causing both pilots to temporarily lose control of their aircrafts. I don't have to tell you the odds they beat in getting safely to the ground."

"And I'm telling you my coordinates were correct," she shot back, then paused a moment. "Actually, Mr. Colbourne, I've gone over this and over this." Her voice was more controlled, but the electric intensity underlying each word betrayed the cost. "And I don't think the Liberty and the AirWest did connect."

"So just what do you think they did collide with?" he demanded. "A UFO?"

"Not in the way you mean, no." She hurried on before he could comment. "As unbelieveable as it may sound, I think they both clipped the primary target."

The Predator simply continued to stare at her. "Let's say for the moment that your . . . scenario is possible." His flat tone indicated what he thought of that probability. "If the primary target had clipped tips with the other planes, it would most certainly have lost control as well, if not crashed. We have no indication of that happening. At the very least, someone on board the Liberty or the AirWest would have seen the primary target if it was as close as you said in your report."

"There was dense cloud cover, not to mention the fact that it was the middle of the night. So any sight reports would be suspect."

He leaned forward and rested his elbows on the desk. Why did she get the impression that he was going in for the kill?

"Before you dig yourself in any deeper, Ms. Burke, perhaps you should be aware that both of the captains and their first officers aren't completely convinced that the primary target ever existed."

Dane Colbourne watched her closely. Surprise, then anger showed openly on her face. There was not even a flicker of fear or vulnerability. He didn't know what in the hell to make of her.

She shot to her feet and planted her fists on the edge of the desk. "What do you mean they don't think there was a third plane?" Her shoulder-length brown hair swung forward with the abrupt movement, her eyes were bright with indignation. They were blue, he now realized. A clear, brilliant blue, like the sky at twenty thousand feet. "Of course there was a third plane! It sure as hell was on my display! Check the tapes if you have to. But it was there. And it must have flown right between the Liberty and the AirWest."

If it hadn't happened hours ago, Dane would have questioned whether or not those few glasses of champagne he'd had at the wedding reception had actually impaired his thinking. Her theory was crazy. And he'd have to be crazy to believe it. But his thinking wasn't impaired. And one thing he was very clear on, was that when it came to one Ms. Adria Burke, nothing she said or did was going to be taken lightly.

Damn but he wanted some aspirin. Raking a hand through his hair, he worked harder for a patient tone than he could remember having to do for some time. One look at the stubborn set to her jaw told him that even if he dredged it up, it wasn't likely to hold for long.

"Your theory leaves too much unexplained," he said shortly.

Adria rolled her eyes and made a very unladylike sound of disgust. And Dane suddenly—impossibly—found himself fighting the urge to smile. He was used to mowing people down with his confidence and certainty, used to getting the job done and done right. Only now did he realize just how exhilarating a worthy adversary might be. If this wasn't so damn serious, he might actually enjoy going to head to head with her.

She blew out a deep breath, causing the wispy hair

fringing her forehead to flutter up, then settle down in complete disarray.

He watched her, waiting and wondering what she'd do or say next. Wondering why he felt such an odd sense of anticipation. Why in the hell he didn't step in and bring this to his customary finality with a few well chosen and completely unchallengeable statements.

"Listen," she said finally. Didn't she know just how completely she had his attention? "I don't see why we're even arguing about this. I mean, the ARTS III tapes contain all the display data. They'll prove what was there. That the third plane *was* there."

She really was amazing. She'd been through a harrowing experience, and while the ending had ultimately been a happy one for the passengers and crew, her job was still on the line. She had to be wiped out. And yet, she sat there and defended her actions in a rational and calm manner.

Well, mostly calm anyway. He lowered his head and scanned his notes again, stifling for the second time the urge to smile.

He'd looked at her job file and had to admit he was damned impressed. She'd passed her written test on the first try, which wasn't so unusual, but her scores had been perfect. Then she'd been one of the lucky ones to pass her security clearance check quickly and had landed a plum—and highly unusual—assignment straight out. She'd obtained her FPL—full performance level—rating there in what had to be record time. It normally took four years, she'd done it in three. And the fairy tale career had continued when her first FPL assignment had been a level five facility. D.C.'s Metropolitan.

Any suspicions about how she might have landed it would have been put to rest by her work record. She'd been here two years and her performance rating was outstanding. Or at least, it had been up until recently. It was that tiny section of her work history that he'd focused on. Had to focus on.

According to her file, she'd been reprimanded twice in the last six months. Neither time for anything remotely as serious as the collision, and both times, she'd shouldered the blame entirely with no argument, no excuses offered.

Even now, it seemed to him she was as concerned with determining what really happened as she was with clearing her name. His strengths as an investigator were the same ones she'd obviously developed as a controller. The ability to remain cool and detached no matter how extenuating the circumstances. To focus on the facts at hand.

In his case that included going over and over every detail of an incident until any flaw in logic or action was uncovered and analyzed. And all the cold hard facts in this case—not to mention the flaws—all pointed at the controller sitting directly across from him.

He couldn't ignore the regret he felt, but he didn't let it come through when he spoke. "They are making copies of the ARTS tapes as we speak. The data printout will include everything from the time you took over control of your position. I'll also be going over the voice and data tapes from both flights."

He stood and massaged the bridge of his nose, his headache having settled into a slow steady throb. "I will probably have additional questions. Please leave a number with Mr. Beck where you can be reached and try to stay accessible."

Several moments of silence passed, then she stood. "That's it?" she asked with disbelief.

Not hardly, he wanted to respond, but didn't. Dane swallowed a groan as his shoulder and neck muscles began to compete with the pain in his head. He had long hours ahead of him with no sleep in sight. Instead of the usual rush of anticipation he felt when he took on a new investigation, he simply felt tired. And confused. He never felt confused.

"I'm very thorough, Ms. Burke." He locked gazes with her once more. "And I'm damn good. I'll find out happened. No matter what."

She opened her mouth as if to speak, but only huffed out a small sigh of resignation. It bothered Dane more than he cared to admit just how curious he was to know what she'd been about to say.

She lifted her purse from the chair and dug inside. Pulling out a small pad and pencil, she hastily scribbled something, then tore the sheet off and handed it to him. "My home phone number," she told him. "Though as thorough as you are, I'm sure you have it there in those notes somewhere. As you probably also know, I'm not union, so I've been placed on temporary leave until you file your report with Mr. Beck and the FAA. There's a machine on that line in case I'm not home."

She was such an easy read. He knew she was dying to ask what his early conclusions were. But she wasn't going to. Even though she understood that whatever final decision was made would be done largely on the basis of his report. He was very probably holding her entire career in his hands. A career that, up until just recently, she'd obviously worked damn hard to make a stellar one. He couldn't deny that he admired her silence.

It wasn't until he tried to tuck the card in the inside pocket of his jacket that he remembered he was still wearing his tuxedo.

When he'd been beeped at the reception, the only phone available had been in the limo that had brought some of the wedding party. Once he'd called in and been briefed, his only concern had been getting to the airport. He hadn't taken the time to go home or even drop in at his office to change.

He caught a glimmer of humor in her eyes before she carefully masked it.

"I, uh, was at a wedding reception. My sister's," he said, wondering even as he offered the explanation why he'd done so. He wasn't used to explaining himself, preferring to let his work speak for him. That he hadn't, until this moment, given any thought to how people perceived him on a personal level, did little to ease his uncustomary awkwardness. When she didn't say anything, he felt foolish. He stuffed the card into the top folder. "I'll let you know if I find out anything to support your theory."

"Thank you," was all she said. Clearly she didn't think he was going to look too hard for that support. That rankled. But he'd be damned if he'd offer any further assurances. She'd learn about him soon enough.

Then a spark of something he couldn't put a name to flashed in her eyes. "Nice tux." She reached out to straighten his rose. "Hot pink is definitely your color." Then she turned and left the room without another word.

THE EDITORS' CORNER

If it's love you're looking for, you've come to the right place. Our TREASURED TALES IV romances brim with excitement and adventure as your favorite authors add a sexy contemporary spin to everyone's favorite classics. Each of these wonderful novels features memorable characters finding love in the unlikeliest of places. TREASURED TALES IV is your invitation to join them on the most romantic journey of all.

Goldilocks is more than a match for three big, bad bears in Debra Dixon's **BAD TO THE BONE**, LOVESWEPT #774. He's a brand of danger she's never risked, with the most unforgiving pair of blue eyes that ever stared into her troubled soul, yet Jessica Daniels insists she doesn't have the answers to Detective Sullivan Kincaid's questions about a missing person. But the innocent act doesn't fit with the way the mysterious brunette arouses Sully's suspicions—and his most forbidden desires. Debra Dixon delivers a once-in-a-lifetime read with this powerfully emotional, savagely sensual, yet utterly romantic novel.

Romance Writers of America president Janis Reams Hudson delights with **ANGEL ON A HARLEY**, LOVESWEPT #775. Just as Whitney Houston confounds Kevin Costner in the instant classic movie THE BODYGUARD, Faith Hillman isn't at all what Dalton McShane expects when he faces the woman who claims she is carrying his child. And Dalton McShane isn't what she's been expecting either. Right name, wrong guy . . . Clearly, Faith is a woman betrayed—big time. Then, an act of violence makes it obvious that if ever there is a woman in need of a knight in shining armor, Faith is it. Weaving a story of forbidden passion and potent seduction, of unspoken dreams and second chances, Janis Reams Hudson celebrates the sweet power of enduring love and its healing magic.

MIDNIGHT HEAT, LOVESWEPT #776, is the provocative finale to Donna Kauffman's THE THREE MUSKETEERS trilogy. They call him The Predator, the investigator who never leaves a case unsolved, and now Dane Colbourne has set his sights on her! Adria Burke knows her quick response prevented a tragic midair collision, but Dane wants evidence that proves her case—and his fierce, hot look tells her he wants her just as much. When men who'll risk anything finally taste irresistible danger in the arms of women who can't help getting a little too close to the flame, there's no one better to write their stories than Donna Kauffman.

Last but by no means least, Faye Hughes shines

with star power in **WILD AT HEART,** LOVE-SWEPT #777, inspired by the timelessly appealing movie IT HAPPENED ONE NIGHT. In Faye's delicious homage, Jake Wilder crashes a party looking for scandal and maybe a chance at redemption, but when Maggie Thorpe drags him into a closet to elude his pursuers, what else could he do but kiss her breathless? Her untamed heart recognizes a kindred spirit beneath Jake's outrageous charm, but once they team up to expose a shady deal, the sinfully sexy reporter must convince the rebel heiress they are meant to be partners in passion forever. Sparkling with wicked fun and seductive as a Southern drawl from a bad boy's lips, this tantalizing tale of love in close quarters shows just why Faye Hughes is a fan favorite every time!

Happy reading!

With warmest wishes,

Beth de Guzman   Shauna Summers

Senior Editor   Associate Editor

P.S. Watch for these Bantam women's fiction titles coming in February: *New York Times* bestselling author Iris Johansen weaves her special brand of magic with **LION'S BRIDE,** a sizzling new novel of passion, danger, and sensuality. **SEE HOW THEY RUN** is a gripping novel of romantic suspense in the tradition of Joy Fielding by acclaimed talent Bethany Campbell, and Elizabeth Elliott follows up her spectacular Fanfare debut of THE WARLORD with **SCOUNDREL**—a story of passion in a world of war and intrigue where the greatest danger of all is in daring to love. Be sure to see next month's LOVE-SWEPTs for a preview of these exceptional novels.

*To enter the sweepstakes outlined below, you must respond by the date specified and
follow all entry instructions published elsewhere in this offer.*

DREAM COME TRUE SWEEPSTAKES

Sweepstakes begins 9/1/94, ends 1/15/96. To qualify for the Early Bird Prize, entry must be received by the date specified elsewhere in this offer. Winners will be selected in random drawings on 2/29/96 by an independent judging organization whose decisions are final. Early Bird winner will be selected in a separate drawing from among all qualifying entries.

Odds of winning determined by total number of entries received. Distribution not to exceed 300 million.

Estimated maximum retail value of prizes: Grand (1) $25,000 (cash alternative $20,000); First (1) $2,000; Second (1) $750; Third (50) $75; Fourth (1,000) $50; Early Bird (1) $5,000. Total prize value: $86,500.

Automobile and travel trailer must be picked up at a local dealer; all other merchandise prizes will be shipped to winners. Awarding of any prize to a minor will require written permission of parent/guardian. If a trip prize is won by a minor, s/he must be accompanied by parent/legal guardian. Trip prizes subject to availability and must be completed within 12 months of date awarded. Blackout dates may apply. Early Bird trip is on a space available basis and does not include port charges, gratuities, optional shore excursions and onboard personal purchases. Prizes are not transferable or redeemable for cash except as specified. No substitution for prizes except as necessary due to unavailability. Travel trailer and/or automobile license and registration fees are winners' responsibility as are any other incidental expenses not specified herein.

Early Bird Prize may not be offered in some presentations of this sweepstakes. Grand through third prize winners will have the option of selecting any prize offered at level won. All prizes will be awarded. Drawing will be held at 204 Center Square Road, Bridgeport, NJ 08014. Winners need not be present. For winners list (available in June, 1996), send a self-addressed, stamped envelope by 1/15/96 to: Dream Come True Winners, P.O. Box 572, Gibbstown, NJ 08027.

THE FOLLOWING APPLIES TO THE SWEEPSTAKES ABOVE:

No purchase necessary. No photocopied or mechanically reproduced entries will be accepted. Not responsible for lost, late, misdirected, damaged, incomplete, illegible, or postage-die mail. Entries become the property of sponsors and will not be returned.

Winner(s) will be notified by mail. Winner(s) may be required to sign and return an affidavit of eligibility/release within 14 days of date on notification or an alternate may be selected. Except where prohibited by law, entry constitutes permission to use of winners' names, hometowns, and likenesses for publicity without additional compensation. Void where prohibited or restricted. All federal, state, provincial, and local laws and regulations apply.

All prize values are in U.S. currency. Presentation of prizes may vary; values at a given prize level will be approximately the same. All taxes are winners' responsibility.

Canadian residents, in order to win, must first correctly answer a time-limited skill testing question administered by mail. Any litigation regarding the conduct and awarding of a prize in this publicity contest by a resident of the province of Quebec may be submitted to the Regie des loteries et courses du Quebec.

Sweepstakes is open to legal residents of the U.S., Canada, and Europe (in those areas where made available) who have received this offer.

Sweepstakes in sponsored by Ventura Associates, 1211 Avenue of the Americas, New York, NY 10036 and presented by independent businesses. Employees of these, their advertising agencies and promotional companies involved in this promotion, and their immediate families, agents, successors, and assignees shall be ineligible to participate in the promotion and shall not be eligible for any prizes covered herein.   SWP 3/95

DON'T MISS THESE FABULOUS
BANTAM WOMEN'S FICTION TITLES